She stepped into the

At the edge of the terrace, out of sight of anyone inside, she called softly, "Jake?"

"Over here."

She moved toward his voice, finding him in the deeper shadows of the garden. He wore jeans and a T-shirt, and his hair was damp, as if he'd just come from the shower. For the longest moment he stared down at her. "God, you're beautiful."

He touched her necklace with his fingertips, and Hope felt the thud of her pulse against her throat. Strange that after all this time Jake could still do that to her.

"I used to see you this way sometimes when I'd be here visiting. I'd watch you come out of the house and I'd think how perfect you looked. How much you belonged here."

"But you were wrong," Hope said softly. "I never really fit in here. I didn't even want to." She took his hand, drawing their linked fingers up to her cheek. "I'm a cop's daughter, Jake. And I should have been a cop's wife."

His eyes closed briefly. "Do you know how long I've waited to hear you say that?" He drew his knuckles down her cheek. "When this is over..." He said nothing else, just stared down at her with a look that captured her breath.

"I'd better go," Hope said, "before someone comes looking for me. I'll be back when I can."

"You do that," he said, his gaze dark and intense. "Because I'll be waiting."

Dear Reader,

When my editor asked me to turn an idea I'd recently pitched to her about a thirty-year-old kidnapping into a three-book series, I was intrigued—and stumped. How could I create three separate mysteries, and three separate love stories, within one big mystery—i.e., the kidnapping? Each book would need its own hero and heroine, its own cast of characters and suspects, and its own—hopefully—satisfying conclusion.

As I considered the possibilities, I began to realize just how many lives would be affected by such a tragedy—the woman whose father was convicted of the crime and the man whose father became a legend for solving the case (The Hero's Son); the kidnapped child's twin brother and a dangerous impostor (The Brother's Wife); and finally, the little girl—all grown up now—who was in the nursery at the time of the kidnapping and who has been haunted for over thirty years by what she may have seen that night (The Long-Lost Heir).

I hope you enjoy THE KINGSLEY BABY series and come to care as much for the characters as I did. Follow their stories next month in The Long-Lost Heir.

Happy reading,

Amanda Stevens

The Brother's Wife
Amanda Stevens

Harlequin Books

TORONTO • NEW YORK • LONDON
AMSTERDAM • PARIS • SYDNEY • HAMBURG
STOCKHOLM • ATHENS • TOKYO • MILAN
MADRID • WARSAW • BUDAPEST • AUCKLAND

For Steven, Lucas and Leanne

ISBN 0-373-22458-3

THE BROTHER'S WIFE

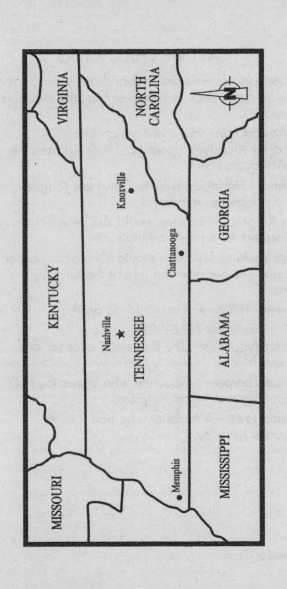

CAST OF CHARACTERS

Hope Kingsley—Is her husband really dead, or has he come back to keep her from the man she loves?

Jake McClain—His investigation into Andrew Kingsley's death got him fired from the police department.

Michael Eldridge—Is he the long-lost Kingsley heir or a dangerous impostor?

Iris Kingsley—How far would she be willing to go to protect the family's reputation?

Pamela Kingsley—She would like nothing better than to see her own son inherit the Kingsley fortune.

Jeremy Willows—He would do anything to get in Iris Kingsley's good graces.

Victor Northrup—The Kingsleys' attorney and closest friend.

Jonas Thorpe—A hoodlum who knows the truth about the real Adam Kingsley.

Simon Pratt—A mobster who had it in for Andrew Kingsley.

Prologue

"You look like a desperate man." The woman slid onto the barstool next to Andrew Kingsley and crossed her long, sleek legs.

He glanced at her appreciatively. She wore a short black dress that looked very expensive, very classy, and very sexy. Her eyes were blue, her hair so blond it was almost white, her oval face pale and flawless.

Her features gave her the illusion of softness, but there was something about her eyes, something simmering beneath the misty blue surface that belied her angelic appearance.

Another time she would have held Andrew's undivided attention. But not now. Not with the argument he'd had earlier with Hope still ringing in his ears. After ten years of marriage, she wanted a divorce, and there wasn't a damn thing he could do about it. God knew, she had her grounds.

The woman next to him swiveled on her barstool until the toe of her shoe brushed the back of his leg. "Well, are you?" she persisted.

"Am I what?"

"A desperate man."

He shrugged. "I guess you could say that."

She leaned toward him, so close he could smell her perfume, something dark and sensuous. Very seductive. She smiled knowingly. "Let me guess. Your wife kicked you out and you lost your last dime at the track."

"You must be psychic," he muttered.

She smiled again. "Not really. But I *am* very perceptive. My name is Carol, by the way."

Andrew motioned to the bartender looming nearby. "Carol needs a drink."

The bartender gave her an approving once-over. "What'll it be?"

"White wine."

He brought her wine and another whiskey for Andrew. Scowling, Andrew stared at the drink. He was driving tonight. He usually limited himself to one, no more than two drinks. This would be his fourth, but hell, it wasn't every night a man lost his wife, his fortune, and maybe even his life, if he couldn't figure out a way to pay off his gambling debts. He needed this drink badly.

Carol ran a manicured finger around the rim of her wineglass. "So why don't you tell me your troubles? Maybe I can help."

"I don't think you can help me get my wife back," he said. He didn't think anyone could do that.

"You might be surprised what I can do."

"Look. You're a very attractive woman—*very* attractive," he added, his gaze slipping over her. "And I'm sure most any man in this bar would love to tell you his life story. But right now, I'm really not in the mood for conversation."

She didn't seem the least bit offended by his brush-off. In fact, Andrew wasn't sure she'd heard him. Her gaze was glued to the TV mounted over the end of the bar, and she seemed to be listening closely to a news broadcast, something about a policy decision the President had recently made.

"Interesting story," she murmured.

Andrew lifted his glass. "I wouldn't know."

"Don't you keep up with politics?"

"No more than I have to."

She frowned, as if his answer displeased her. Hesitating, she said, "Have you ever heard of an organization called the Grayson Commission?"

Andrew shrugged, bored with the conversation. "Can't say as I have."

"It's a group of powerful men and women, some from the business world, some from the political arena, and some from—shall we say?—the underworld, who have banded together to affect government policy from within. They're always on the lookout for viable political candidates—people who, if elected, would be sympathetic to certain causes."

"Meaning?"

"Meaning you."

He stared at her in astonishment and laughed. "You're kidding, right? You don't even know me." When she didn't respond, his laughter faded. "Like I said, I'm not the least bit interested in politics."

"But you *are* a Kingsley."

An alarm went off inside him. "How do you know who I am?"

"Everyone in Memphis knows the Kingsleys. I've read all about you. Your family has a long and illustrious tradition in politics. Thirty years ago, your grandmother managed to get your father elected governor when his supporters had all but deserted him."

"If you know your history as well as you say you do, then you know public sympathy put my father in office," Andrew told her. "The election swayed in his favor when my twin brother was kidnapped, and believed to be killed."

"Don't underestimate your grandmother, Andrew. We don't. She's a very powerful woman to this day. With the commission's backing and hers, you could become a very strong candidate."

Andrew still didn't know whether to take her seriously or not. The notion of him running for office was ludicrous. "Even if I were interested in politics—which I'm not—you're forgetting one thing. I hardly have the background that would endear me to voters."

"That wouldn't be a problem."

"What do you mean, that wouldn't be a problem? Of course, it would be." His father's hasty second marriage had almost derailed his gubernatorial bid before it ever got started. And compared to Andrew's indiscretions, a hasty second marriage was nothing. *Nothing.*

"The Grayson Commission has people in the organization who can give you any kind of background they want you to have."

"No one can do that anymore," Andrew said. "There isn't a public-relations firm in the country that can hide anything from the media these days." Now that the police were involved, it was only a matter of time before some nosy reporter found out about his association with Simon Pratt, a well-known mobster in these parts. Andrew cringed when he thought of the headlines.

"Believe me, that wouldn't be a problem."

Her persistence was beginning to annoy him. "Look, I don't know who you are or what kind of scam you're trying to pull here, but I have no interest in politics, the Grayson Commission, or much of anything else right now. All I want is to be left alone. Okay?"

He turned to his drink, but her hand on his arm drew his gaze back to her. She leaned toward him. "You might want to reconsider, Andrew. One word from me and your debts would all disappear."

His eyes narrowed. "How do you know about my debts? Who the hell are you?"

"Simon Pratt is a very dangerous man, from what I hear. He's been known to break the arms and legs—or worse—of those who default on their loans. I'd hate to see that happen to you."

Andrew looked at her in disgust. "That's what this is about, isn't it? You work for Pratt. This is some kind of sick game he's orchestrated to torment me."

Her gaze deepened. "This is no game, believe me. I'm offering you the chance of a lifetime. Think about it, Andrew. How many people in your position get the opportunity to start over? To have mistakes from their past erased as if they never happened?" She lifted her wineglass and stared at him over the rim. "You could become the kind of man your wife always wanted you to be."

For a moment, Andrew wanted to believe her. A tiny flicker of hope ignited inside him, then died. He shook his head. "You're crazy. You don't know anything about me or my wife. Our marriage is over. Finished. And so is my life."

"It doesn't have to be that way."

"Yes, it does. Trust me, I'm as good as dead in this town."

The woman's smile turned mysterious. "Funny you should say that."

The bar had become more crowded as the evening wore on. Someone bumped into Andrew's back, and he turned, scowling.

A man wearing sunglasses said, "Sorry, pal."

Andrew shrugged and swiveled back around. Carol smiled. "Well," she said, "if we can't do business, we can at least part as friends, can't we?" She clinked her glass against his. "Here's to second chances."

"Here's to nothing," he said. Which is what he would have left, once Jake McClain, a police detective with an ax to grind, got through with him. Picking up his glass, Andrew downed the contents.

At first the whiskey ignited his stomach, then settled into a nice, warm glow. He glanced at the blonde. Her features seemed softer now, and exquisitely feminine. She saw him watching her, and slowly, very deliberately licked her lips.

"Let's get out of here," she said. "Find some place where we can talk."

"About politics?" His tongue seemed thick all of a sudden.

She shook her head. "No. About you and me."

The comfortable numbness from the whiskey wore off too quickly. His head began to pound, and he thought he was going to be sick. "I don't feel well."

"Here." She took his arm and helped him up. "You need some fresh air."

She guided him through the throng of people to the door, held it open for him, then helped him across the parking lot to his car.

"Better call a cab," he muttered, leaning against the door. "Don't think I can drive."

She fumbled in his pocket. "I'll take you home."

No, Andrew thought. What if Hope saw him with another woman? But then in the next instant, he realized it didn't matter. Hope was gone for good this time. Or soon would be. Back to Jake, unless he could think of a way to stop her.

He let the blonde help him into the passenger side, then watched through slitted eyes as she crawled behind the wheel. She started the powerful engine, expertly shifted into gear, then tore out of the parking lot like a woman fleeing for her life.

The bar was on a secluded road, several miles from Memphis, near the small town of Shepherd. Andrew liked to go there because no one ever recognized him. But the blonde had known him, and had somehow known he would be there. Because of that, the deserted highway seemed particularly menacing to him now.

Who are you? he tried to ask her again, but no words came out. The pain in his head became excruciating. He slumped against the door.

"Andrew?"

When he didn't answer—couldn't answer—he heard her mutter, "Damn. It wasn't supposed to happen like this."

What wasn't? he tried to scream. *What have you done to me? Stop the car! Let me out of here!*

"You're going to be all right," she told him. "Believe me, this is all for the best."

Propelling himself away from the door, Andrew lunged toward the steering wheel and grabbed it. Carol screamed, trying to shove him away. For several moments, they struggled. Then the car careened off the road, out of control as they missed a curve, and Carol screamed again. She threw up her arms to protect her face as the car plowed down an embankment, straight toward the trunk of a tree.

The last thing Andrew heard was the sickening crunch of metal against wood. The last thing he saw was the splatter of blood against the windshield. The last thing he thought was that this time, Jake had won.

The game was finally over.

Chapter One

The car reminded him of a sleek, red bullet—low-slung, fast, and dangerous. Jake McClain shoved a tiny plant into the freshly dug hole, then stood to admire the clean, smooth lines of the Viper as it tooled around the sharp curves in the drive leading up to the Kingsley mansion.

Next to Jake, his father, who had been the gardener at the Kingsley estate for as long as Jake could remember, was on his knees, still bent over the flower bed in front of the house.

Each hole had to be precisely dug, each plant had to be gently, almost lovingly placed inside, and then the dirt had to be carefully tamped in place. His father's movements were slow, methodical, precise, and Jake bit back an oath. At this rate, they would be out here all night.

"Pop," he said, trying to temper his impatience. "Whose car is that? I haven't seen it around here before."

Gerald McClain glanced over his shoulder as the vehicle came into view, then he returned to his work. "It doesn't concern you. Stay out of the Kingsleys' business."

Jake scowled. Ever since he'd moved in with his father a couple of weeks ago, the two of them had been at each other's throats. Jake had known it would be this way. He and his father were both too strongly opinionated not to have disagreements, but what else could he do? His father had recently suffered a mild heart attack, and there was no one else to watch out for him, to make sure he didn't overdo. The Kingsleys sure as hell wouldn't.

Unfortunately, however, since Jake had sold his house to cover the legal fees he'd incurred fighting his dismissal from the police department, his father had decided that Jake was destitute and had nowhere else to go. He thought he was doing Jake a favor by letting him move back home.

It was true Jake was down on his luck right now, but that wouldn't last long. He'd already opened a private investigation firm and was actively seeking clients. And in the meantime, if his living on the Kingsley grounds afforded him the opportunity to continue looking into Andrew Kingsley's death, Jake figured he could put up with a little harassment from his father.

From all indications, Kingsley had been into something pretty heavy before his death, and Jake had been determined to find out what it was, to bring down Andrew Kingsley if it was the last thing he ever did. Instead, Kingsley had died in a car crash, and Jake had been booted off the police force for instigating an unauthorized investigation—an infraction that should have warranted a reprimand or a suspension at worst; but Jake had been dismissed because Iris Kingsley was still a powerful woman in these parts.

She didn't like having her grandson's memory tarnished, especially by the likes of Jake McClain.

He wondered if she was up there now, staring down at him with smug satisfaction that he had finally been put back in his place.

The red Viper pulled around the circular drive and stopped in front of the house. Jake couldn't see the occupant of the car, but his instincts—and his father's attitude—told him that something was definitely going on. He shielded his eyes from the sun and waited for the driver to emerge. When no one got out, he turned back to his father.

"Pop," he said. "You know everything that goes on around here. Who is that?"

Gerald glanced up at him. "Leave it alone, Jake, and get back to work. You're supposed to be helping me today."

"We've been out here all day without a break," Jake reminded him. "Why are you being so secretive?"

His father heaved a weary sigh. He sat back on his knees, rubbing his gloved hands along the tops of his thighs. "All right. I know you. You won't give me a minute's peace until I tell you. Word has it around the staff that a man claiming he might be Adam Kingsley is coming to see Miss Iris and Mr. Edward today. I reckon that's him."

Jake glanced down at his father in shock. "You're kidding."

"He contacted Miss Iris yesterday."

"*Yesterday?* You mean she's agreed to see him this quickly? He must have told her one helluva story."

Adam Kingsley, Andrew's twin, had been kidnapped from the mansion when the boys were only three years old. Until recently, the authorities had believed that Adam was dead. Shortly after the kidnapping, his body had been recovered from a shallow grave near the Kingsley estate and buried in the family plot. But everything changed a few months ago when the real kidnapper had finally admitted to the crime, thirty-one years after he'd taken Adam.

An ex-cop named Raymond Colter confessed that he and a woman had kidnapped the child for ransom, and then the woman had vanished with the boy. According to Colter, Adam Kingsley was still alive the last time he saw him, and his story was borne out when the body was exhumed. DNA testing proved conclusively that the remains were not those of Adam Kingsley but of another little boy named Johnny Wayne Tyler, who had been murdered by his stepfather.

Colter's story kicked up a storm of controversy, not just in Memphis, but all over the country. And as expected, an army of impostors claiming to be Adam Kingsley had descended upon the family. Their attorney, Victor Northrup, had set up a task force within his law offices to handle and investigate each claim. To Jake's knowledge, not one of the would-be heirs had made it past Northrup's assistants.

Until now.

As Jake stood watching, the door of the mansion opened and Iris Kingsley appeared in the doorway. He hadn't seen the woman in months, and he was amazed at how much she'd aged since he'd spoken with her after Andrew's death.

Always thin, she looked frail enough now to be blown away by a puff of wind. Even from a distance, Jake could see the deeply creviced face and the clawlike hand that clutched the front of her black jacket. She hardly seemed strong enough to wield the kind of power that had gotten him fired from the police department, but Jake knew her appearance was deceiving. At eighty-five, Iris Kingsley was still as tough as nails. And still very powerful.

A shadow stirred behind her, and Iris turned to say something over her shoulder. Then the shadow stepped forward, into the sunlight, and Jake's breath caught in his throat.

Hope.

She was still living in the Kingsley mansion. Jake had harbored some notion that after Andrew's death, she might move out, might even go back to her old neighborhood, where her mother still lived. But such hadn't been the case. She was still a Kingsley, and Jake would be a damned fool to ever forget that fact.

As with Iris, the months since Andrew's death had taken a toll. Hope looked too thin and too pale in the subdued navy dress she wore. Her straight, brown hair was pulled back from her face, giving her features a gauntness that wasn't altogether unattractive. She had the appearance of a woman who needed taking care of, and Jake wished like hell he wasn't having the thoughts he was having.

She didn't notice him at all. He was just a workman in the gardens, not worthy of her or Iris Kingsley's attention. Both of their gazes were glued to the car, and in a moment, the door opened and a man climbed out.

The car was parked at such an angle that the women couldn't see his face, but Jake could. The man glanced in his direction. Their gazes collided, and the impact was almost like a physical blow. Jake stood for a moment, too stunned to react.

The man looked exactly like Andrew Kingsley. *Exactly.*

The blue eyes, the dark hair, the arrogant set of his features—all the same.

Even the contemptuous glance he threw Jake was enough to send a cold chill down Jake's spine. It was almost as if his nemesis had come back to life. But that was impossible. Andrew Kingsley was dead, and this man…this man…

No wonder Iris had agreed to see him so quickly. He must have sent her a picture of himself. His amazing resemblance to Andrew would naturally pique her interest.

With a curious little smile, the man turned and started walking toward the mansion, his shoulders squared, his gait confident. Jake shifted his gaze to Hope, studying her expression. He saw her eyes widen with the same shock he'd experienced seconds earlier.

Then, as the man drew closer, shock turned to wonder, and Jake's heart twisted unexpectedly. He saw her lips move, forming Andrew's name, as she took a tentative step toward the stranger.

"MY NAME IS MICHAEL Eldridge. But, of course, you already know that." The stranger smiled down at Iris, then turned to encompass everyone in the room, his dark blue gaze resting for an instant on Hope.

Her face heated as she remembered the moment outside when she'd said Andrew's name and started toward him only to stop short when he'd stared at her with eyes that held not the slightest bit of recognition.

He was seated on the white brocade sofa beside Iris. Grouped around him were Edward Kingsley—Andrew's father—Edward's wife, Pamela, and her son, Jeremy Willows. Hope remained on the fringes of the conversation, still unable to resolve the strong emotions she'd felt on first seeing Michael Eldridge. There had been shock, of course, and a sense of wonder that some miracle was taking place right before her eyes. But there had also been something else lurking in her subconscious, a darker emotion she didn't want to explore.

"Tell us about yourself, my dear," Iris invited. She wore black, as she had since Andrew's death, but beneath the severely tailored jacket, she'd donned a blue silk blouse that added softness to her features. Her coloring had always been striking, with her dark blue eyes, pale complexion, and thick, snowy white hair. Her posture was still as straight as a ramrod, her bearing shamelessly arrogant.

The man beside her smiled. "There isn't much to tell, I'm afraid. As I told you when I called, I'm a stockbroker in Houston. I was raised in a series of foster homes after my mother abandoned me when I was five years old. I don't remember her. I don't remember anything about my real parents at all, and to be honest, I've never been all that curious. I guess I just thought if they'd wanted me..." He broke off, shrugging.

"Well, anyway, after your grandson died, someone showed me his picture in the paper. I was...shocked, to say the least. And I felt an immediate...connection with him. I can't really explain it. It wasn't just because we looked so much alike. It was more than that.

When I stared at his picture, I felt as if I'd...*known* him. And I felt this deep, terrible sense of loss...."

No one said anything. They were all spellbound by his story, Hope included.

He cleared his throat, as if made self-conscious by his confession. "I started making some inquiries to try and learn all I could about your family. You may find this hard to believe, but I had no idea who the Kingsleys were. When I found out that you all are practically royalty in these parts..." His smile turned self-deprecating. "Well, I don't mind admitting, it was a bit daunting."

"I can imagine," Pamela Kingsley murmured, smoothing the skirt of her turquoise silk dress. Sunlight caught the diamonds around her throat and both wrists as she perched on the arm of her husband's chair, one hand resting on his shoulder. "It isn't every day one learns he might be the sole heir to a considerable fortune."

Michael stared at her, forcing her to meet his gaze. "I know what you're thinking, and I don't blame you. You only have my word that I didn't come here to lay claim to your family's fame and fortune. But I've actually done quite well for myself. I don't really need your money, and I've never been one to crave the limelight. The reason I'm here is because—" He broke off again, seemingly at a loss for words. Then he turned back to Iris. "The reason I'm here is because I couldn't stay away. Can you understand that?"

She smiled and took his hand. "Yes, I believe I can."

Hope watched the exchange worriedly. For all her wealth and power, Iris was as fragile as a wounded bird. She was extremely vulnerable right now, and Hope knew she could easily be hurt.

It was for precisely that reason that Hope had remained on here after Andrew's death. In the days and weeks following the accident, Iris had begged her not to move out of the mansion. She was Iris's last tie to Andrew, and her despair had been so great that Hope was afraid to upset her any further. To make matters worse, Iris's doctor had warned the family that her heart might not be able to take any more stress.

And so Hope, realizing it was the worst thing in the world she could do for herself, had agreed to stay with Iris for a little while longer. But days had turned into weeks, weeks into months, and here she was, no closer to moving out and starting a new life for herself than she had been the night she'd asked Andrew for a divorce.

The night he died.

As the voices droned on around her, Hope turned to look out the window, which faced the front lawn and gardens. Her gaze took in the lush, manicured grounds, the colored fountains, the marble sculptures, and she realized with something of a shock, that she was searching for Jake McClain.

Ever since he'd moved in with his father, she'd caught glimpses of him on the grounds. He'd been out there earlier, when Michael had first arrived, and Hope had seen him out of the corner of her eye.

It had taken all her willpower not to turn and stare at him. He'd been working in the gardens, and Hope could still picture the way he looked, standing there shirtless in the sunlight, his low-slung jeans hugging his lean hips and thighs.

With an effort she turned her attention back to the

gathering, and started. From across the room, Michael Eldridge was staring at her so intently, it almost took Hope's breath away.

My God, she thought. *He does look exactly like Andrew.*

From his vantage, he had an unobstructed view of Hope and the window behind her. As his gaze deepened, Hope had the strangest feeling that he knew exactly what she'd been doing—whom she'd been looking for—and he didn't like it. Not one bit.

A shiver raced up Hope's spine at the way his thick lashes hooded his blue eyes, giving them a dark intensity that was disturbingly familiar.

Their gazes clung for a long moment as Hope's heart pounded and her mind whirled in confusion. Who was this man who looked enough like her dead husband to *be* him? Who was this stranger who seemed to know her innermost thoughts, her deepest, darkest secrets?

After what seemed an eternity, the man's gaze shifted to Edward, who was speaking quietly to Iris.

Edward was a younger, weaker version of his mother, with the same white hair, the same deep blue eyes, and the same arrogant demeanor. But where his mother had retained her slender physique, her elegant beauty, Edward's good looks, at sixty, had succumbed to the desecration of his vices. His eyes were shadowed and puffy, his jowls sagged, and his once-muscular body had grown soft and cumbersome.

To look at him now, one would never have guessed he had once been a powerful man in this state, a governor over thirty years ago who had been on the short list to run for vice president. But then, after two terms as governor, he had retired from politics, much to

Iris's keen disappointment, and had discreetly gone about the business of destroying himself.

All this Hope had learned from Andrew, who had never been close to his father. And he'd always despised his stepmother, Pamela, and her son, Jeremy Willows. "Parasites," he'd called them in kindness. "Bloodsuckers," when he was particularly aggravated by something one of them had said or done.

As Hope glanced at Pamela and Jeremy now, she wondered what they thought of this new development—a man looking exactly like Andrew appearing out of the blue to claim his rightful place in the family; a man who might very well be the sole Kingsley heir.

A position Jeremy had wanted for himself, Hope reflected, taking in the deep scowl on his face as he stood at the fireplace, away from the rest of the family. He looked the part of heir-apparent in his custom-made suit and expensive Italian loafers, but he was still an outsider, even after all these years, and no one knew that better than Jeremy.

"We'll have to have some sort of verification," Edward was saying. "There are tests...."

"Edward." Iris's tone held a note of warning, as if she were telling her son, *Stay out of this. I'll handle it.* "It's premature to be speaking of tests. This visit is so we can all become acquainted."

"No, he's absolutely right, Mrs. Kingsley," Michael said earnestly. "The sooner we find out the truth, the better for all of us." He turned to Edward, the man who might be his father. "I'm perfectly willing to submit to any tests you want, sir. Hypnosis, polygraph, even DNA. Although that might be difficult, considering we would need a sample of Adam's DNA.''

Hope, who had remained quiet and introspective the entire time, surprised herself now by speaking up. ''It might not be as difficult as you think. Since Andrew was Adam's identical twin, his DNA would be a virtual match, wouldn't it?''

Michael's blue gaze met hers, and for just an instant, Hope felt the man's intensity, his displeasure, then it was gone, replaced by a wan smile. ''But Andrew's dead. That's how I came to realize I might be his brother. As I said, I saw his picture in the paper and saw how much we looked alike.''

''Yes, I know,'' Hope said, refusing to concede to the man's melancholy charm as easily as Iris had. ''But Andrew went in for a physical the day before he died. The lab might still have his blood specimen. And if not, I believe the hospital took a sample the night he died.''

''If that's true, Victor would be able to make all the necessary arrangements,'' Edward said.

''Why not let Jeremy look into it?'' Pamela suggested.

''I'd be happy to do whatever I can,'' Jeremy murmured.

''Nonsense,'' Iris declared. ''Victor is like family, and he has a great deal of experience in these matters. Not to mention his discretion,'' she added unkindly, but didn't see, as Hope did, Jeremy's angry blush at her insinuation. Iris had already turned back to Michael. ''I'm so glad you came here today. You have no idea how much better I feel, just seeing you.''

He smiled at her. ''You're exactly the way I pictured you after speaking with you on the phone, Mrs. Kingsley.''

"Call me Iris, please. 'Mrs. Kingsley' sounds so formal, and I do hope we'll become friends. Andrew and I were very close, you know. He was a wonderful man.''

Hope started to turn away, not wanting to hear Iris's glowing memories of Andrew, which were so different from her own recollections. But her gaze met Michael Eldridge's, and slowly, almost imperceptibly he winked at her.

Hope stared at him in shock. The action was so much like Andrew that for a moment, the thought crossed her mind again that he *was* Andrew, perpetrating some elaborate hoax.

AFTER MICHAEL LEFT, Hope went up to have tea with Iris in her sitting room. As she settled onto a green silk settee, Hope thought again how much she loved this room. So much of the house seemed oppressive and gloomy, with the high-vaulted ceilings, the dark wood paneling, and the ornate, antique furnishings. But this room was sunlit and cheerful, done in gold, ivory and subtle shades of green.

A discreet knock on the door was followed by the entrance of a uniformed maid carrying a silver tea service on an ornate tray. The tea was poured, and Iris took a tentative sip from a delicate porcelain cup, then dismissed the maid with a satisfied nod.

As if in silent accord, the two women set aside their cups and turned to face each other. Iris had removed her suit jacket, and the blue silk blouse brought an unexpected sparkle to her eyes. She even wore a hint of blush, Hope noticed, or were the roses in the older woman's cheeks natural? Iris had been so pale and listless since Andrew's death. The vital woman sitting before Hope now seemed almost a stranger.

Before Hope had a chance to speak, Iris lifted her hand, which appeared steadier than it had in months. "I know what you're about to say. Edward has already been in to see me, and I suspect Jeremy will be up before dinner. If he can muster the courage," she added scornfully. "Let me assure you, as I did my beloved son and his wife, that I have no intention of making Michael Eldridge my heir until we have conclusive proof he is my grandson."

Hope smiled at the woman's forthrightness. No need beating about the bush with Iris. "I'm glad to hear that. Although I'm less worried about your will than I am about your heart. I don't want to see it broken again."

The old woman's face crumpled for a moment, as she remembered Andrew's death. She turned away until she'd regained her composure, then once again met Hope's gaze. "Do you think he's another impostor?"

Hope shrugged. "I don't know. There've been so many. Especially since Andrew died."

Iris drew a long, weary breath. "But none of them looked the way he does. Did you see his eyes, Hope? He's a Kingsley. I'd stake my life on it."

That was exactly what Hope was afraid of. "I think we should reserve judgment until we find out more about him."

"He's agreed to the DNA testing," Iris reminded her.

"Yes, and hopefully, that'll give us the proof we need. But those kinds of tests sometimes take weeks,

I understand. In the meantime, you could have an investigator check him out—''

''No.''

Hope looked at the older woman in concern. ''Why not? Surely you want to find out all you can about this man.''

Iris's chin lifted in the arrogant, stubborn manner the family had seen too little of in the past few months. ''I don't want a stranger poking around in our affairs and compromising our privacy. I want this kept as quiet as possible. You know as well as I do what the media would do with a story like this. No matter what kind of life Michael has led, they would twist things to make it sound sordid, perhaps even criminal. Look at what they tried to do to poor Andrew. It wouldn't be fair to Michael. Besides...'' Her blue eyes grew even more determined. ''I already know the truth about him. All I have to do is look at him.''

Hope leaned forward, taking Iris's hand in hers. ''I know he looks like Andrew. Enough like him to be his twin brother. But looks can be deceiving.''

''But he's *exactly* like Andrew. The way he walks. The way he talks, laughs, smiles. Oh, Hope.'' Iris's grip tightened with surprising force on Hope's hand. ''Don't you see? It's as if Andrew's come back to us.''

THAT NIGHT HOPE couldn't sleep. She tossed and turned, unable to get the image of Michael Eldridge out of her mind. His striking resemblance to Andrew had brought back so many painful memories. She couldn't forget the way Andrew had looked the last time she'd seen him, the anger and hurt in his blue eyes as she'd lashed out at him. The cruel set of his mouth as he'd smiled down at her, taunting her.

In the stillness of the night, their last argument seemed to echo against the walls of the bedroom they'd shared for nearly a decade. Unable to stand the torment any longer, Hope got up and crossed the room, opening the French doors to the mild April night. She stepped onto the balcony that overlooked the rear gardens, trying to distance herself from the room and from the memories.

And from the guilt.

The sky was still and clear, with a sprinkling of stars and a full moon that silvered the aquamarine surface of the swimming pool. The scent from the wisteria near her window wafted on the evening breeze, and through the trees, Hope could see the flickering light from the groundskeeper's cottage where Jake's father lived. Where Jake was staying. She wondered if he was there now.

She closed her eyes as Andrew's last words came back to haunt her.

"You've never gotten over him," he'd accused her. "Why don't you just admit it? You still love him. That's why you want a divorce."

"This isn't about Jake," Hope had said wearily, placing a stack of sweaters inside the open suitcase on their bed. Andrew sat across the room from her, sprawled in a chair by the window. His dark, brooding gaze followed her every move. "It never was about Jake, except in your mind. We could have had a good marriage, Andrew. I did love you. Once. But you never gave us a chance."

She'd seen the truth of her words flicker in his eyes, replaced almost immediately by the darkness that had become all too familiar lately. "Like hell. Don't blame me for this. And don't try to pretend you're not running to *him*. How long has this little affair been going on behind my back?"

Hope met his gaze. "I haven't seen Jake in years. You know that."

"Liar." Andrew sprang up from the chair and strode across the room toward her, as graceful and dangerous as a panther. "He was here the other day. I know you saw him."

"He came to see you, not me. I didn't even talk to him."

But Andrew had seemed not to hear her. He'd already drawn his own conclusions, and nothing she could say would make a difference to him. It never had.

Hope closed the lid of the suitcase and snapped the locks. "There's no point in trying to reason with you when you're like this. I'll call you in a few days when I get settled."

"Don't give me that damned icy brush-off of yours. I'm sick of it." Andrew grabbed her suddenly and spun her around to face him. "Do you think I'll let you just walk out of here like this? There's no way I'll let you go to him. I won't let him win."

Hope flung off his hand and glared up at him. "That's all I am to you, isn't it? The winner's prize in this stupid competition you've always had with Jake McClain. You're not a child anymore, Andrew. You don't have to be jealous of Jake any longer."

His mouth curled in outrage. *"Jealous?* Of the gardener's son?"

"He's always been more than that and you know it. That's why you hate him."

His brows rose in derision. "He's a *cop,* Hope. Which is exactly why you broke off your engagement to him, remember?"

"Yes," she said quietly. "I remember."

"He's nothing," Andrew spat.

He's more than you'll ever be, Hope thought, then realized in horror that she'd spoken the words aloud.

Something changed in Andrew's eyes, a resolution that was almost as frightening as his anger. "So. The truth finally comes out."

She couldn't have said anything that would have wounded Andrew more deeply. Jake McClain had always been a thorn in her husband's side. The two of them had been playmates as children, fiercely competitive even back then—Andrew with the Kingsley wealth and power backing him, and Jake with nothing more than a chip on his shoulder and a fierce determination to someday get away from the shadow of the Kingsley mansion.

In spite of all the advantages Andrew had grown up with, it was Jake who had become something of a local hero, excelling in athletics in both high school and college. It was Jake who had known exactly what he wanted in life and attacked his ambitions with a vengeance, while Andrew had drifted from day to day, restless and discontented, with no aim in life other than to own the fastest cars and to be seen with the most beautiful women.

It was Jake Hope had fallen in love with, and for that, Andrew had never forgiven her.

"I won't give you up," he warned.

"You don't have a choice," she retorted. "Our marriage has been over for a long time. Just let it go."

"I won't let him have you." Andrew tried to touch

her, but Hope jerked away. His eyes darkened. "I'll see you both dead first."

She stared up at him, hating the sight of him, hating herself for the life she'd given up ten years ago. Her anger, always hidden beneath the surface, bubbled over, hot and fierce, before she could stop it. "I'd rather *be* dead than to stay married to you!" she screamed.

He looked stunned for a moment, then his smile chilled her to the bone. "Careful what you wish for, Hope."

He turned and strode from the room, slamming the door behind him. Within moments, she heard his car roaring down the driveway, and all Hope could think was that she was glad he was gone. She wished she would never have to see him again.

"Careful what you wish for, Hope."

As those images once again stormed through her, Hope shivered. The breeze had picked up, stirring the scent of the roses. The sky, clear moments before, was now dotted with clouds. A lacy filigree covered the moon, deepening the shadows in the garden beyond the pool. Suddenly, Hope had the strangest sensation that she was being watched from the darkness.

"Jake?" she whispered, but the night remained ominously silent.

Unsettled by her thoughts, Hope turned and sought the shelter of her bedroom, closing and locking the French doors behind her.

Chapter Two

The morning after Michael Eldridge's visit dawned warm and sunny, and when Hope came downstairs, she found Iris breakfasting on the terrace. She was alone at the table, reading the paper and sipping her coffee.

"Where is everyone?" Hope sat down and unfolded her napkin.

"Jeremy has already left for the office, I believe, and my son and his wife are sleeping in. As usual."

Even though Edward and Pamela had been married for over thirty years and had lived in the same house with Iris for most of that time, she never referred to her daughter-in-law as anything other than "my son's wife." Iris hadn't approved of Edward's second marriage, coming such a short time after his first wife had died of cancer when Andrew and Adam were three years old, and because of her disapproval, Pamela was not and never would be considered a Kingsley, just as her son would never be Iris's heir.

A maid appeared, bringing fresh coffee and orange juice. Iris laid the paper aside and glanced out at the gardens. "Gerald is at work early this morning, I see."

"He always is," Hope said, following Iris's gaze. Her heart thudded against her chest when she saw that Jake was with his father. They were working near the reflecting pool, tearing down an old rock garden that Iris had decided a few days ago was an eyesore.

"Hope," she said. "Go out there and stop them."

Hope glanced at her. "What? Why? They're doing exactly what you told them to do."

"I'm aware of that. But I've changed my mind. The rock garden was Andrew's favorite place to play when he was a little boy. I don't know what I was thinking. Please go tell Gerald I wish to see him."

Hope rose, knowing that arguing would be futile. When Iris made up her mind, there was no talking her out of it.

Leaving the terrace, Hope walked down the sloping lawn toward the rock garden. Morning sunlight glinted off the surface of the reflecting pool, temporarily blinding her. She shaded her eyes as she approached Jake and his father.

What had once been an artful arrangement of rock and plants was now in complete disarray. The two men must have been working for hours already, because the job was almost completed.

As Hope watched, Jake, his muscles bulging with the weight, picked up one of the last remaining stones and carried it to a wheelbarrow. He'd taken off his shirt, and a sheen of sweat glistened along his backbone. Hope felt something stir inside her, a warning that told her to state her business, then get away from there as fast as she could, before she had time to remember.

But it was too late, because when Jake turned back around he saw her. Their gazes held for the longest moment, and it flashed through Hope's mind that here was a man she had once been engaged to. A man she had once hurt very deeply. A man who despised the path she had chosen for her life.

As if reading her mind, Jake studied her for a moment, taking in the designer dress she wore, the gleam of gold at her wrist and throat, and then wordlessly he turned his back on her and resumed his work.

Hope felt as if he'd slapped her. A part of her wanted to hate him for it even as another part of her realized she probably deserved it. The last time she and Jake had met face-to-face was when he'd come to question her after Andrew's death.

In the throes of guilt for the terrible things she'd said to her husband on the night he died, Hope had lashed out at Jake, accusing him of trying to exact revenge on a dead man. But in the weeks and months that followed, Hope had come to realize that Jake had been right. Her husband had been a man of secrets. Dark and deadly secrets.

And now another man claiming to be Andrew's twin brother, a man who seemed to have secrets of his own, had come back into their lives just when Hope thought she might be able to put the past behind her. Now she wondered if she would ever be able to do that.

"Mr. McClain?"

Jake's father glanced up and smiled. "Miss Hope. What brings you down here?"

Was it Hope's imagination, or had he cast a furtive glance toward his son?

Jake didn't look up from his work, but Hope saw his expression darken at the way his father had addressed her. At one time, Gerald McClain had almost been her father-in-law, and now here he was, addressing her as though she were the mistress of the manor.

Hope had never felt as uncomfortable with her position in the Kingsley household as she did at that moment. She'd never felt as if she belonged here, amid all this wealth and grandeur, but now she realized she didn't belong in her old world, either.

Where, exactly, did she belong?

Jake stopped what he was doing and glared at her. "Well? Was there something you wanted, Hope?"

There wasn't the slightest bit of subservience in his tone. In fact, the way he said her name was almost an insult.

Hope lifted her chin. "I came to have a word with your father."

Gerald removed his gloves and slipped them in his back pocket. "What can I do for you?"

"Mrs. Kingsley would like to see you. Something about the rock garden. I'm afraid she may have changed her mind," Hope added apologetically.

Gerald's face showed not the slightest bit of anger or resentment over the news. Instead he said to Jake, "Just keep working. We'll have to remove everything and start over anyway."

Hope lingered for a moment, unsure whether or not she should strive for a note of civility before she left. Jake glanced up, looking as if he wanted to say something to her, but changed his mind with a shrug. He nodded in the direction of the terrace. "Looks like you have company."

Hope glanced over her shoulder. Michael Eldridge, wearing dark glasses and an Italian-designer suit, stood on the terrace, staring at the gardens. When he saw Hope, he lifted his hand and waved.

Hope waved back, but she found that she was shivering in the warm April sunlight. She turned back to Jake. "I guess I'd better get back."

"Yeah." Something dark flashed in Jake's eyes. "Looks like he's waiting for you."

WHEN HOPE RETURNED to the house, Iris announced that the two of them would accompany Michael to a private clinic where Victor Northrup had already made arrangements for a sample of his blood to be taken and sent to Dr. Henry Wu, a leading forensics expert in Boston. Two samples of Andrew's blood, one provided by his private physician and the other by the Shepherd police, would be sent separately.

Dr. Wu had been the one to discover that the remains in Adam Kingsley's grave were not Adam's, so it seemed fitting that he be the one to perform the DNA tests now on the man who might be the *real* Adam.

All the way to the clinic, Hope noticed that Iris never took her eyes off Michael. It was as if the man's face had mesmerized her, and no wonder. In spite of her uneasiness about him, Hope found herself fascinated by the man as well. His resemblance to Andrew was uncanny, but it wasn't just his physical appearance that intrigued Hope. His mannerisms, the way he smiled, the way he looked at her were all reminiscent of her dead husband. *Too* reminiscent. Could brothers, even identical twins, who had been raised apart grow up to be so very much alike?

The only difference Hope had been able to discern so far was a scar at Michael's left temple. She gazed at that scar on the way to the clinic, wondering how he'd gotten it.

A blond receptionist looked up from her work as they entered the lobby of the clinic. The woman was strikingly beautiful with the pale, flawless skin of a Scandinavian ancestor and eyes as blue as the icy North Sea. She smiled at them, but her eyes remained cool and appraising as she waved them toward the waiting room.

In a few moments, a nurse came out and ushered Michael into an examination room, where his blood would be drawn, labeled, and sent to Dr. Wu. Every possible precaution would be taken, they were assured, to prevent any kind of contamination that might compromise the tests.

While they waited, Iris busied herself making calls on her cellular phone, and Hope flipped through a magazine. Once she looked up to find the receptionist gazing at her intently.

Instead of glancing away, as most people would do when caught staring, the blonde continued to gaze at her until Hope was the one who looked away. When she glanced up again, the woman had gone back to her work, but the incident left Hope mystified. It was almost as if the woman knew her from somewhere, but Hope didn't think that was possible. The blonde's features were very distinct, not the kind even another woman would forget.

In a few moments, Michael came out of the examination room, rolling down the sleeve of his shirt and fastening the cuff. The doctor followed, assuring them the sample would be sent to Dr. Wu promptly, and that they should have the results in a few weeks.

"Well," Michael said, slipping into his jacket. "I guess all we can do now is wait."

Iris smiled as she allowed him to help her to her

feet. "We can do more than that," she said. "We can all three go somewhere and have lunch. It'll be a celebration."

"What are we celebrating?" Michael asked indulgently, tucking her arm through his.

Iris's face looked radiant as she gazed up at him. "That you've come back home to us. That we can all be a family again. Isn't that so, Hope?"

Hope nodded, unable to speak. A tremor of dread coursed through her. Somehow this man who looked so much like her dead husband had already insinuated himself into their lives.

And from the proprietary look in his dark blue eyes as he gazed first at Iris and then at Hope, he was going to do everything in his power to keep it that way.

THAT AFTERNOON, while his father made plans for the new rock garden—a task Jake decided wouldn't unduly stress him—Jake went back to the groundskeeper's cottage on the edge of the Kingsley estate to shower and change into clean jeans and a white cotton shirt before heading into town to check in at his new office.

The building was near the airport, in an area heavily populated by convenience stores, nightclubs and strip joints—a location that was hardly conducive to attracting the big corporate accounts Jake was interested in, but all he could afford at the moment.

A receptionist in the lobby answered phones for most of the small offices in the building, and as Jake approached her desk, Deanna Logan glanced up with a hopeful smile. It was just before five, and she looked as if she were getting ready to leave for the day. She slipped the gold compact and lipstick she'd been using back inside her purse.

"Hi, Jake. I didn't think you were coming in today."

Jake shrugged. "I have some paperwork I need to get caught up on."

"I tried to beep you earlier." Deanna's brown eyes were soft and curious. "But you didn't call back."

"I forgot and left my beeper at home. What's up?"

"I have some messages for you."

Jake arched a brow. "Bill collectors?"

She grinned. "Not all of them. One sounded like he might be a potential client. Said he's looking for someone to do a background check for him."

Jake took the pink message slips, thumbed through them until he found the one he wanted, then looked up with a frown. "He didn't leave a name or number?"

Deanna shook her head, and the permed waves in her hair rippled in the fluorescent lighting. "Said he'd call back later."

Right, Jake thought, wadding the messages into a tight ball. More likely he'd gone on to the next name in the Yellow Pages, which brought up an interesting question. McClain Investigations wasn't listed in the phonebook yet. How had the man found out about him?

"If he calls back before I leave, I'll put him right through," Deanna said helpfully.

"You do that." Jake headed for the elevator.

"Jake?"

He glanced back over his shoulder. Deanna blushed as she curled a strand of brown hair around one finger.

"I was wondering. You wouldn't, uh, like to have a drink or something after work, would you?"

Jake grimaced inwardly. Deanna was a nice girl, and he didn't want to hurt her feelings. He knew she'd developed a crush on him since he'd opened his office, but she was just a kid, probably no more than twenty-two or twenty-three. The last thing she needed was to get involved with the likes of him, and the last thing he wanted was an entanglement of any kind.

"Thanks for the offer," he said. "Best one I've had all day. But I have to get to that paperwork."

She blushed again and glanced down at her desk. "Some other time, maybe."

"Yeah." He escaped into the open door of the elevator and punched the button for the third floor.

McClain Investigations was located at the end of a long corridor, with several accounting and insurance firms in between. Most of the businesses were one-man or one-woman operations like his, but a few had their own clerical staff, and as Jake walked down the hall to his office, there was a brief but intense exodus toward the elevator as workers headed for home or happy hour.

He unlocked his door and flipped on the light switch. The office was small, barely accommodating his desk, two filing cabinets—which did double duty as fax-machine and coffeemaker stands—and two brown leather chairs, worn but still in good condition. The view from those chairs was somewhat obstructed by the computer monitor on his desk, but Jake had neither the space nor the extra cash for a separate computer desk.

A small storage room contained office supplies,

surveillance equipment, and a cot that Jake occasionally used when he stayed late at the office.

Turning on his computer, he settled back in his chair and sorted through the mail that had been inserted through the slot in his door.

"Occupant, occupant, occupant," he muttered, tossing one unopened envelope after another into the trash. The bills he shoved into his top drawer, out of sight.

As always when he had nothing else to do, and sometimes when he did, Jake opened the Andrew Kingsley file and perused his notes, wondering how much, if anything, Hope knew about Andrew's association with Simon Pratt. How much she'd known about her husband's gambling and drinking and, if the rumors were true, his infidelities.

A knock on the door scattered Jake's thoughts, and he looked up with a frown, wondering if Deanna had come to try and change his mind about the drink. He hoped not, because in his present mood, he might not let her down so easily this time. Hell, he might not let her down at all, and that would be a big mistake. For both of them.

"Come in," he called.

The door opened and a man with silver hair and a deeply bronzed face stepped inside. He looked to be in his late sixties or early seventies, tall and thin with a regal bearing and expensive attire that suggested he might be one of the well-heeled corporate clients Jake had been hoping for. But Jake knew that wasn't the case. He recognized the man.

"Hello, Jake." The deep, cultured voice contained only the barest trace of a Southern accent, the gray eyes only a hint of the contempt he felt for Jake. "I suppose you're surprised to see me," said Victor Northrup.

"Don't tell me." Jake sat back in his chair and eyed Northrup warily. "You were in the area and thought you'd drop in. Which really means, you're here to check out my new office and report back to Iris Kingsley."

Victor smiled. "She has no idea I'm here, and I'd like to keep it that way."

Something in his tone intrigued Jake, though he had no intention of letting Victor Northrup know that. Northrup was not only Iris Kingsley's closest friend, but also her attorney. He'd been instrumental in getting Jake fired from the department, and Jake still carried a grudge. He didn't like the man, and what was more, he didn't trust him.

Without being invited, Northrup sat down in one of the leather chairs and crossed his legs, apparently at ease. But a slight twitch at the corner of his left eye suggested he might not be as relaxed as he wanted to appear.

Jake came around the desk to lean against the edge, so that the computer monitor wouldn't be an obstacle. He didn't want to miss one single flicker of the man's expression.

"So you've gone into the P.I. business, have you?" Northrup glanced around the shabby office. "Business is booming, I see."

Jake folded his arms. "You don't hear me complaining, do you?"

Northrup smiled. "You should be. You haven't had a client since you opened this office four weeks ago. Your reputation precedes you."

"Thanks to you and Iris Kingsley."

Northrup shrugged. "I know you believe otherwise, but Iris and I had nothing to do with the review board's decision to dismiss you."

"Like hell," Jake said. "Let's just cut to the chase here, okay? What do you want?"

Northrup reached inside his pocket, and Jake automatically tensed, his training still deeply ingrained. But instead of a weapon, Northrup withdrew a photograph and handed it to Jake. "Who would you say this man is?"

Jake took the picture and glanced down at the familiar blue eyes, the dark hair, the arrogant smile. He returned the picture to Northrup. "He looks like Andrew Kingsley, but I assume, since you bothered to ask, that he's the man claiming to be Adam Kingsley."

Northrup was clearly startled. "You know about him?"

"I was helping my father in the gardens when he arrived at the mansion yesterday."

Northrup sat forward in his chair, his expression tense and alert. "Did you get a good look at him?"

Jake shrugged. "Fairly so."

The gray eyes hardened almost imperceptibly. "What did you think? Did he look like the man in this photo?"

Jake stared at Northrup in surprise. "Are you telling me you haven't met him yet? I thought your office handled all claims against the Kingsley estate."

"We do. I've seen the man's picture, and I've spoken with him on the phone. But I haven't met him in person yet."

"Then how did he connect with Iris? And with Edward?" Jake added, though everyone knew Iris was the head of the family. If rumors were true, Edward was hardly in any shape to choose which socks to wear each day, let alone which Adam Kingsley wannabe to interview.

Northrup's features hardened. "He was shrewd enough to bypass my office and go directly to Iris. He sent her a picture of himself, and the resemblance to Andrew was so great, she agreed to see him. In fact, she offered to fly him from Houston to Memphis in the Kingsley jet, but he declined. He told her it wouldn't be right to spend Kingsley money on him until they know for sure he's Adam. Iris was very impressed by this."

"I can imagine," Jake said dryly. He sat on the edge of his desk, gazing down at Victor Northrup. "But what does any of this have to do with me?"

"I'm coming to that," Northrup said, hesitating. "As Iris's attorney, but more importantly as her friend, my job is to protect her interests. At any cost. For all we know, this man is a very clever impostor who has managed to circumvent the background check my office would have conducted on him if not for Iris's intervention."

"Can't your office conduct the investigation now?" Jake asked.

Northrup shook his head. "It's now become very complicated. Iris, you see, has convinced herself this man is her long-lost grandson. He's agreed to a DNA test, but we won't have the results for weeks. In that length of time, a professional con man can do a great deal of damage, both financially and psychologically. It's the latter I'm most worried about. Iris is extremely vulnerable right now. If she continues to believe this man is her grandson, and then finds out weeks later that he is not, the result could be devastating.''

"I understand," Jake said. "But I still don't see why your office can't at least run a background check on him."

Again Northrup hesitated, steepling his fingers beneath his chin. "Iris doesn't want an investigation of any kind. She's made her position very clear. She wants to believe this man is her grandson for as long as possible. If I find out that he isn't...if I'm the one to break the news to her—"

"I get it," Jake interrupted. "She might want to shoot the messenger."

The piercing gray eyes met his. "That's where you come in. I want you to investigate this man, leave no stone unturned, but I don't want anyone to know that I've hired you."

"What if I find out he's an impostor?" Jake asked. "How are you going to convince Mrs. Kingsley?"

"You get the proof," Northrup said. "I'll worry about dealing with Iris. Do we have an agreement?"

Jake had a feeling that making a deal with Victor Northrup might be akin to striking a bargain with the devil. He wasn't about to rush into anything. He knew Northrup hadn't.

"Let me think about it overnight and I'll let you know tomorrow."

Northrup seemed surprised by Jake's hesitancy, but he shrugged. "Fair enough," he replied, rising to leave. "I'll expect to hear from you first thing in the morning. We can go over the details then."

When Northrup was at the door, Jake said, "One more thing."

Northrup turned.

"Why me? There are dozens of qualified investigators in this city. You have to know how Mrs. Kingsley feels about me."

"That's precisely why I chose you." Northrup's expression remained unfathomable. "You aren't afraid of Iris Kingsley, and from what I've been able to gather, you don't mind getting your hands dirty if the situation warrants it."

FROM HER CAR, HOPE watched Victor Northrup leave Jake's building and head her way. She slumped in her seat, not wanting to be seen. Iris had made her wishes clear, and if Victor saw Hope here, he might put two and two together and figure out she'd come to hire Jake to investigate Michael.

Come to think of it, what was Victor doing here? Hope wondered, lifting her head slightly to see if he'd passed by her car yet. She couldn't imagine that he'd been visiting a client in this area of town. Could he have been here to see Jake, too? Had he also gone against Iris's wishes and hired a private investigator to check into Michael's background?

But why Jake? Northrup's law firm had several private investigators on the payroll at any given time. Why would he not use one of them? Unless, of course, he was afraid Iris might get wind of the investigation. But whatever his motive, Hope knew he had thought out his alternatives carefully. Victor Northrup was not an impulsive man.

Although he had been close to the Kingsleys for years and Iris and Andrew had trusted him implicitly with both their private and business dealings, Hope didn't really like Victor. There had always been something about him that was just a little too smooth.

A little too polished. When he had brought her the news of Andrew's death, his condolences had sounded almost practiced, as if he knew the right things to say, but lacked the emotion to make them convincing.

Hope watched him get into a silver Rolls-Royce and pull away from the curb. She waited until he was out of sight, then got out of her car and crossed the street to Jake's building. The receptionist had already left for the day, so Hope studied the directory mounted on the wall near the entrance to locate Jake's office.

The elevator lifted her to the third floor, and when the doors slid open, Hope's stomach knotted with nerves. What if he wouldn't see her? He'd been so cool to her this morning, and there was no reason to think his attitude might have changed in a few hours. Ten years of bitterness lay between them, after all, and as Hope stood outside his office door, poised to knock, every one of those years came crashing down on her.

Before she could change her mind, she lifted her hand and rapped on the door, then opened it without waiting for him to answer.

Chapter Three

"Hope?" Jake cocked his head, gazing at her warily as she stood in his doorway. She wore a white suit that made her look crisp and clean and very expensive. *Untouchable* was the word that came to mind. "Is something wrong?"

She looked uncertain for a moment, as if she'd somehow been picked up and transported to his office through no will of her own. Like Dorothy landing in Oz. Her light brown hair was pulled back and fastened at her nape, emphasizing her high cheekbones, the delicate arch of her brows. "No. Nothing's wrong. I'd like to talk to you if you have a minute."

"What about?"

She paused, glancing around his office as if to make sure they were alone. "You were at the house yesterday when Michael Eldridge came to see the Kingsleys."

"The man claiming to be Adam Kingsley, you mean." Jake leaned against the desk, crossing his feet at the ankles. He waved her to one of the leather chairs in front of his desk, and Hope sat down. "He was there again this morning, wasn't he?"

Hope nodded. "He isn't exactly claiming to be

Adam Kingsley. At least, not yet. But Iris is convinced that he is. He bears an amazing resemblance to Andrew.''

"Yeah. I saw him." He'd also seen Hope's face yesterday when she'd seen him. For a moment, it had been as if she'd thought Andrew had come back from the dead, and her unbridled reaction wasn't something Jake had been able to put out of his mind since.

He gazed at her now, wondering what the hell she was doing here. When he'd seen her just after Andrew's death, she'd barely been civil, but Jake guessed he should have expected that. He'd found out some pretty dark secrets about her husband, and Hope hadn't wanted to believe him.

The two of them had never been able to see eye to eye on Andrew Kingsley. Jake had known Andrew all of his life, had thought him to be an arrogant, selfish bastard, but Hope, from the very first time she'd met him, had thought him charming and sophisticated. A true Southern gentleman. So different from the cops she'd been around all of her life. So different from Jake.

He used to wonder how their lives might have turned out if he hadn't been the one to introduce Hope to Andrew. Jake wanted to believe it no longer mattered, but deep down, he knew that it did. He knew it every time he caught a glimpse of Hope driving up to the Kingsley mansion in her white Jaguar. He knew it every time he saw the wide band of diamonds glittering on her finger and the expensive clothes gracing her slender body.

He knew it now, as his gaze skimmed her familiar features—the lightly tanned complexion, the golden-brown hair, the beguiling violet eyes. It mattered then, and it mattered now, that she had chosen Andrew Kingsley over him.

More than Jake wanted to admit.

She crossed her legs, and he heard the slight rustle of her nylons. Awareness shot through him like a bullet. Hope Sterling was still the most desirable woman he'd ever known. Ten years and a dead husband lay between them, but Jake still found her just as attractive as he ever had. The knowledge made him want to put his fist through a brick wall.

Instead, he stared at her calmly, waiting for her to speak.

"Before I tell you why I'm here," she said, "I'd like to ask you something. Would you tell me why Victor Northrup was here to see you?"

Jake shrugged. "Who says he was?"

"I saw him leave your building right before I came in."

"Lots of people have offices in this building besides me," Jake replied. "The nature of my business is confidential. I don't talk about who comes and goes through that door."

Hope smiled slightly. "I guess I can appreciate that. Especially since I don't want anyone to know I've come here, either. But I have to know whether or not you're working for Victor."

"Why?"

"Because I'd like to hire you myself. To investigate Michael Eldridge."

Jake lifted his brows in surprise. "But you made your feelings about me perfectly clear after Andrew died."

She glanced away. "That was different."

"How? You didn't believe what I found out about

your husband. Why would you believe what I tell you about this guy?''

She studied the purse in her lap for a moment, then her gaze lifted to his. ''Because you don't hold a grudge against Michael Eldridge.''

His voice hardened. ''I told you then and I'll tell you now. My investigation into Andrew's connection with Simon Pratt wasn't personal. I was doing what any good cop would have done.''

''But you weren't just any cop,'' she said. ''And no matter how hard you might have tried, I don't think you could have kept your personal feelings out of your investigation.''

''So what makes you think I can do that now?'' He gave her a long, relentless stare. ''There are other investigators in Memphis, Hope. Why did you come to me, knowing how I feel about the Kingsleys? Knowing how they feel about me?''

She hesitated, as if unsure how far she was willing to go. Then she shrugged. ''Because I know you're good. I know you can't be bought. And because I need to know the truth about this man. As soon as possible.''

There was a desperation in her eyes that intrigued Jake. ''Why not let the Kingsleys handle it? After all, this really doesn't concern you any longer, does it?''

Anger flickered in her eyes before she quickly quelled it. No one else would even have noticed, but after all these years, Jake still knew Hope too well. Ten years had not changed the fact that she still tried to suppress her emotions—and he still didn't want to let her get away with it.

They had been like fire and ice, he and Hope. His temper had always been hot, fierce, quick to explode, while her anger lay frozen beneath the surface, dormant for days, weeks, sometimes months at a time. Maybe even years, he thought, gazing at her now.

"Just because Andrew is dead doesn't mean I don't still care about his family," Hope said. "Iris especially. She's been very good to me, Jake. I don't want to see her hurt. She's very fragile right now."

Somehow "fragile" wasn't a term he could ascribe to Iris Kingsley.

"I know you don't like her," Hope continued. "I know you think she got you fired from the department—"

"I don't think," Jake interrupted bitterly. "I know. That review board had her fingerprints all over it, and you know it."

He saw her knuckles whiten as her fingers tightened on the clasp of her purse. "I honestly don't know what happened," she said. "But I want you to know I had nothing to do with it."

Jake glanced around his shabby office. "Well, that's some comfort, isn't it?"

The anger flashed in her eyes again, and this time she wasn't so quick to suppress it. She stood. "It was a mistake for me to come here. I should have realized—"

"Yeah," Jake said. "You probably should have. But as long as you're here, you might as well finish what you started."

She hesitated. A myriad of emotions flickered over her features, so quickly even Jake was hard-pressed to recognize them. "Maybe you're right," she said. "Maybe it's time we got everything out into the open. Ten years is a long time to carry a grudge, Jake."

"Is that what you think I'm doing?"

"You think I don't see the loathing and disgust in your eyes every time you look at me?" she asked. "You think I don't know how much you hate me?"

"I don't hate you," he said. Although sometimes he wished he did. Especially at night. Lying alone in his bed. Remembering the way things once were. The way things might have been. "I don't hate you," he repeated.

She didn't respond. Walking over to the window, she stared down at the street. Jake wondered what she saw. The overflowing Dumpster in the alley below? A drunk stumbling out of the bar next door?

Great little place you've got here, McClain.

He wondered what Hope saw when she looked at him. A thirty-five-year-old washed-up ex-cop? A man who had been willing to give up everything for the sake of a career he no longer even had? A failure?

Not a very pretty picture, he thought. Not at all what he had wanted or expected of himself. At least Hope hadn't pointed out how badly he needed a client, as Victor Northrup had. Jake guessed he should be grateful to her for that.

Still gazing down at the street, she said, "Ten years ago, I made a decision about my life. About us. I didn't think I could be a cop's wife after what happened to my father. I was devastated by his death, and the thought of losing you the same way...the thought of our friends from the department showing up at my door one night to tell me you were never coming home...to have their wives try to comfort me while secretly feeling grateful it hadn't been *their* husbands who'd been killed..."

She trailed off and drew a long breath. "I knew I wouldn't be able to bear it. So I broke off our engagement. I thought it would be easier that way, but it may have been the worst decision of my life.''

When she turned to face him, her eyes were like drowned violets, and Jake thought, almost in awe, that she looked close to tears. In all the time he'd known Hope, he'd only seen her cry once—the night she'd learned her father had been killed. She hadn't cried at his funeral, and she hadn't cried the day she broke off with Jake. Her resolve on both occasions had been frighteningly final.

But here she was now, ten years later, with tears in her eyes, telling him things he no longer wanted or needed to hear.

But as soon as the thought shot through his mind, he dismissed it. He must have imagined the tears and the remorse, because Hope's eyes now were clear and more determined than ever, with not so much as a hint of regret shimmering beneath the surface.

''The point is...'' she said, walking toward him. She stopped just short of his desk. Of him. ''It may have been the worst decision of my life, and then again, maybe it wasn't. Who's to say what our lives would have been like if I hadn't broken off our engagement. Who's to say we would have stayed together anyway. I've always liked to believe things happen for a reason.''

He wanted to ask her what reason she'd had for marrying Andrew Kingsley, but he didn't think he'd like her answer. So he said nothing. Instead he stood there feeling like a jerk, and he didn't even know why.

''I guess what I'm trying to say is that if I made a mistake ten years ago, it was my mistake to make and I've had to live with the consequences.'' Her chin lifted stubbornly, a gesture that was all too familiar to Jake. "I won't be made to feel guilty about it any longer."

"Is that what you think I'm doing?" Jake asked, his own anger stirring to life. "Trying to make you feel guilty?"

"This thing you have about the Kingsleys—"

"Was there a long time before I ever met you," he finished for her.

"I know," she said. "But can you honestly say you would have gone after Andrew the way you did if it hadn't been for me? Can you honestly say you wouldn't be willing to help me now if I were just Andrew Kingsley's widow and not your ex-fiancée?"

"Who's to say?" Jake retorted, flinging her own words back at her. "The situation is what it is, Hope."

"Ten years is a long time," she said quietly.

An eternity, he thought. Although not all the years since their breakup had been bad ones. In fact, he'd had some pretty damned good times. He'd even come close to getting engaged again, but things hadn't worked out. Unlike him and Hope, however, he and Melanie had managed to part as friends. They still got together occasionally for drinks. So why did he still feel this bitterness toward Hope? Why did he still feel that she'd betrayed him?

If she'd married anyone but Andrew Kingsley, would he still have felt the same way?

Somehow Jake didn't think so, and the realization wasn't one he was particularly proud of. His rivalry with Andrew went back to their childhood, and Hope had somehow gotten caught in the middle. She was still in the middle, even though Andrew was dead, and suddenly Jake saw how his bitterness toward Andrew, toward all the Kingsleys, had affected his life. Was still affecting him.

Hope was right, he thought. Ten years was a damned long time. People changed. He wished to hell he had. But here he was, still blaming the Kingsleys for everything that had gone wrong in his life. Still blaming Hope for marrying a man who could give her all the things Jake could never hope to provide.

"Can I ask you something?"

"Of course," she replied, but her gaze faltered uncertainly.

"Why did you marry Andrew? Was it because you loved him, or because you wanted to punish me for not leaving the department?"

After a split second of indecision, she shrugged. "Maybe it was a little of both," she admitted. "Dad's murder did something to me. I couldn't seem to pull myself up out of the grief, and every time I saw you in your uniform, it reminded me of…his death. Of what could happen to you…" She trailed off and turned away. "I thought if you would just leave the department, everything would be all right. I could put what happened to Dad behind me and we could get on with our lives. When you refused, it was like a slap in the face. Being a cop was more important to you than I was."

"I couldn't understand why you were making me choose between my life's work and you," Jake said, trying to hide the lingering bitterness. "Being a cop was all I ever wanted to do. It wasn't just what I did, but who I was."

"I know that now," Hope said. Her violet eyes lifted to meet his. "I probably knew it back then, but at the time, it didn't seem to matter. All that mattered was making sure I never went through that kind of pain again.''

An image came to Jake now, of the night her father had been killed, of the way he'd held her in his arms while she'd wept bitter tears, while she'd asked him over and over, ''Why? Why? Why?'' She'd clung to Jake desperately in those first few hours of grief, but by the time the funeral was over two days later, she'd already begun to pull away from him. Nothing he said or did got through to her. It was as if she'd erected a stone wall around her heart, a wall Jake didn't have a prayer of scaling unless he took off his badge for good. And that, he hadn't been willing to do. He had his pride, after all.

Pride was damn cold comfort on long, lonely nights, he thought now. But if he had it to do over again, he knew his decision would probably be the same. He wondered if Hope's would be.

''A few months after our breakup,'' she said, ''I ran into Andrew at an art gallery in Overton Square, one of those little avant-garde places you always hated. I was surprised he remembered me. I'd only met him that one time at your father's house, remember?''

Jake nodded grimly.

''We got to talking. He told me he was sorry about my father, and then he took me out for coffee. I didn't think I'd ever see him again, but he started showing up at the school where I taught, waiting in the parking lot for my classes to be over, and then he would take me out to dinner—or to the theater, to all these wonderful places I'd never been to before. He was a very interesting man. Unlike anyone I'd ever known. He was charming and sophisticated and he made me laugh again,'' she finished softly.

And don't forget the money, Jake thought.

''So you fell in love with him,'' he said, struggling to keep his voice neutral.

''I came to love him,'' she said. ''I thought he was exactly what I needed.''

''And was he?''

She glanced away. ''For a while. But then...''

Jake waited for her to continue, but all she did was shrug. ''It doesn't matter anymore. All that's behind me now. I'm only telling you this so we can come to some sort of understanding.''

He smiled ironically. ''That the past is the past?''

''Exactly.'' Her gaze met his again, and for a moment he thought he saw a flicker of uncertainty in her eyes, as if she hadn't quite convinced herself. Then, with that same stubborn resolve he'd come up against more times than he cared to remember, she said, ''So what do you say, Jake? Will you take this case? I don't know what arrangements you may have made with Victor, but I'm willing to offer whatever you want.''

Jake doubted that very much. ''Tell me what you know about this guy. This Michael Eldridge.''

Her features tightened. ''I don't know that much. Only that he says he's a stockbroker from Houston, he grew up in a series of foster homes, and that he looks...very much like Andrew.''

''What was your gut reaction to him?''

Her startled gaze flew to his. ''Wh-what do you mean?''

''I mean, what did your instincts tell you about

him? You think he's the real thing? An impostor? What?''

''I'm not sure,'' Hope said in a voice that didn't sound like hers. If he didn't know her better, Jake would have sworn he detected a note of fear. But why would she be afraid of this man? Hope wasn't Iris Kingsley's heir. She didn't stand to lose a fortune even if this man did turn out to be Adam Kingsley.

So where did her fear come from? Jake mused. And then it hit him. He felt a sinking sensation somewhere in the pit of his stomach. Could it be that Hope was afraid of falling in love with Michael Eldridge? Because he looked so much like Andrew?

Jake stared down at her, and as if she'd read his thoughts, she glanced away guiltily.

''Iris is convinced he's...her grandson,'' she said.

''But what do you think?'' Jake persisted, studying her closely.

''I think he might be,'' she said, again in a tone that left Jake wondering. ''I have to know the truth about him, Jake. I have to find out if he's who he says he is. For Iris's sake,'' she added, though Jake wasn't convinced her urgency stemmed solely from her concern for Iris Kingsley. There was something Hope wasn't telling him about Michael Eldridge, but he knew better than to press. If Hope wanted him to know, she would tell him. If not, she would withdraw even more if he questioned her.

Proceed with caution, Jake told himself, but whether he liked it or not, he had to admit he was hooked. He would take the case, all right, but not just because he needed the money. Not just because it would give him a measure of satisfaction to be going behind Iris Kingsley's back or to tell Victor Northrup what he could do with his offer.

He would take the case from Hope because if she *was* falling in love with this man, Jake wanted to make damn sure she wasn't going to get hurt.

THE TREE-SHADED STREETS of midtown were bursting with color. Pink, fuchsia, and white azalea blossoms hung heavy on thick bushes that crowded the brick facades of post-World War II houses, while wide rows of tulips, jonquils, and hyacinths lined sidewalks and driveways.

As Hope drove past the Memphis State campus, a touch of nostalgia swept over her. Students lingered on the grounds, enjoying the warm, spring day. Couples strolled along the walkways, groups of friends clustered around benches, and a few brave sunbathers, wanting to get a jump start on their tans, lay shivering on blankets and beach towels.

The year her father had been killed, Hope had been a senior at Memphis State, majoring in elementary education. She'd already had a job lined up at Claymore Academy, an exclusive private school near the medical center, to teach kindergarten in the fall, and she and Jake were to be married in late summer.

Stopping at a light, Hope closed her eyes for a moment, letting the bittersweet memories wash over her. She tried to decide how she felt about her meeting with Jake. She'd certainly accomplished what she'd gone there for. He'd agreed to investigate Michael Eldridge, and Hope knew she should be relieved, but she couldn't quite dispel the premonition of dread that had hung over her since Michael had shown up at the mansion yesterday.

Who was he? If he really was Adam Kingsley, then his physical resemblance to Andrew was understandable. But what about his mannerisms? The way he talked, the way he walked. The way he looked at her. How could that be explained?

And why hadn't she told Jake about her secret fear? *Because you'd sound like an idiot, that's why.*

Still, it bothered her that she hadn't been completely honest with Jake. About a lot of things.

She pulled into her mother's driveway, parking her white Jag behind her mother's dark blue Taurus. A pair of white and pink dogwood trees graced either side of the white-brick house, and the same pink-and-white theme had been carried through in the tulip beds and azalea bushes, giving the place a candy-cane effect that had always reminded Hope of something from a fairy tale.

Her mother loved to garden, and as Hope let herself in the front door of the modest house, she thought again how coincidental it was that her mother and Jake's father shared in this common passion. Hope and Jake had once shared a mutual passion also, but it hadn't been gardening, she thought with an inward blush.

Joanna Sterling, dressed in a green-and-white jogging suit and Nike walking shoes, was on the telephone in the kitchen. She was a small, trim buzz-saw of a woman who walked five miles every day, rain or shine. Hope was lucky if she made it to the gym two or three times a week. As she glanced at Joanna's slender physique, the perky haircut, the sparkling hazel eyes, she thought that at fifty-five, her mother was probably in better shape than she was—both physically and mentally.

Joanna held up one finger, letting Hope know she would just be a minute. Her gold wedding band sparkled in the sunlight streaming in through the bay window behind her. Hope glanced down at the wide band of diamonds on her own finger. In ten years, would she still be wearing the ring Andrew had given to her on their wedding day? Somehow the thought made her indescribably weary.

She sat down at the breakfast table and folded her hands in her lap, catching snippets of her mother's phone conversation.

"Could even do the chapel Friday night after the rehearsal if we need to," she was saying. "I'll call everyone this afternoon, get everything organized...."

Her mother was always organizing something. She worked at the local library part-time, was heavily involved in church activities and with her garden club and women's groups. She made Hope tired just listening to her.

"What a nice surprise," she told Hope as she hung up the phone. "I wasn't expecting to see you today." Pouring them both a glass of orange juice from the fridge, she came over to the table and sat down across from Hope. "To what do I owe this pleasure?"

Hope shrugged. "I just wanted to see you, but it sounds like you're busy."

Her mother brushed off her concern with a wave of her hand. "Oh, that. Tilly McIntyre broke her ankle yesterday, poor old thing. Tripped over a loose board on her porch steps. She's been meaning to get it fixed for ages, but you know how that goes. You remember her, don't you, dear? She's been the cleaning lady at Saint Anthony's for years."

Ever since her meeting with Jake, memories had

been churning inside Hope, and now at the mention of Saint Anthony's, yet another one swept over her. She and Jake had planned to get married in Saint Anthony's, just as Hope's mother and father had. Instead, Hope had exchanged vows with Andrew at Saint Mary's, a huge cathedral downtown, in a ceremony carefully orchestrated by Iris.

Hope had even worn Iris's wedding gown, a Chanel original that had been a showstopper in a 1930s Paris fashion show. The gown was exquisite, trimmed with real diamonds and pearls and lace so delicate it looked as if it would melt to the touch. But Hope remembered thinking, as she fingered the silky folds on the day of her wedding, that she would have much preferred the wedding dress Mrs. Jamison, a seamstress who lived three doors down from her mother, had planned to make for Hope.

"Anyway, she's going to be out of commission for several weeks, and I want to make sure the church is spic-and-span for Brant's wedding on Saturday. You are coming, aren't you?"

"Actually, the wedding kind of slipped my mind," Hope said. "A lot's been going on lately."

Her mother's gaze filled with mild reproach. "The Colters are very old friends of ours, dear. I know it would mean a lot to Brant if you were there. And, I'm sure, to Valerie, too," she added, referring to Brant Colter's fiancée.

"What's she like?" Hope asked.

"Oh, she's very nice," Joanna said. "A little on the reserved side, but that's understandable, considering. Hard to imagine the two of them finally getting together with all the obstacles they had to overcome. Her, the daughter of a convicted kidnapper and murderer, and him, the son of the detective who put her father in prison. And then to find out thirty-one years later that her father was innocent, framed by Brant's uncle..." Her mother trailed off, shaking her head in disbelief. "It just goes to show you, that true love always wins out." She took a sip of her orange juice and eyed Hope over the rim. "By the way, you'll never guess who I saw the other day."

Her mother's innocent tone immediately raised Hope's suspicions. "Who?"

"Jake McClain."

Although she had been half expecting to hear his name, Hope's heart did a strange little flip inside her chest. "Oh? Where did you see him?"

"Right outside. I was working in the yard and a truck drove by. Went right past the house at first, then backed up. Jake got out and came over to say hello. Said he just happened to be in the neighborhood, but I think he was checking on his house, making sure the new owners were taking care of it. He loved that place." Her mother shook her head sadly, but her eyes never left Hope's face. "It was such a shame, what the department did to him."

Hope remained silent, although she knew her mother was waiting for her to say something. When she didn't, Joanna continued, "There was talk that Iris Kingsley got him fired, you know."

Hope sighed but still said nothing. What was the point?

But her mother wouldn't let it rest. "You surely don't condone what she did."

"I don't know that she did anything," Hope said. "I know you don't care for Iris. Few people do. But she's always been very good to me."

"And I'm grateful for that. But Iris Kingsley doesn't do anything without asking for something in return."

"She's never asked anything of me."

Her mother's gaze narrowed on her. "Then why are you still living in that house?"

"We've been over this before," Hope said wearily, tired of having to justify her actions to everyone, including herself.

"You may not see her manipulations," her mother warned. "But I certainly do."

Frustration erupted inside Hope. "It's not like she's holding me prisoner, for God's sake. I'm a grown woman, Mother. Capable of making my own decisions. I'll move out when I think the time is right."

"The time will never be more right that it is now," her mother insisted. Her eyes filled with worry. "I don't trust her, Hope."

"I know you don't. You didn't trust Andrew, either."

"With good reason."

"Maybe so," Hope conceded. "But you never gave him a chance because you never forgave me for not marrying Jake."

Her mother lifted her chin stubbornly, an action that reminded Hope of herself. *The apple doesn't fall far from the tree,* her father used to say fondly. "Well, since you brought it up, I'll just come right out and say it. Jake is a good man, Hope. He didn't deserve the way you treated him."

Hope put a hand to her forehead. "We've been all through this, too, Mother."

"Yes, we have," she agreed. "And in all these

months since Andrew died, I haven't once said 'I told you so.'"

"Thank you," Hope said dryly.

"But I can't hold back any longer. You broke off with Jake because you didn't want to be widowed like I was. I told you then, there are no guarantees in life. I told you it was better to have the years, no matter how few, that God gave you with the man you loved than to live with a lifetime of regrets."

"Mother—"

"It's been five months since Andrew's death, Hope. You need to get away from the Kingsleys and start a new life for yourself. You're still young. You can still get married again and have that family you always wanted."

Hope didn't like the direction the conversation was headed in. "I don't intend to ever marry again," she said firmly. "And, Mother, understand this. I won't put up with any of your matchmaking tactics. Is that clear?"

A guilty blush tinged Joanna's tanned cheeks. "I never said a word—"

"You didn't have to," Hope said. "I can read you like a book. And I know that's where all this talk about Jake is leading. But it's not going to happen."

Her mother opened her mouth to protest, then clamped it shut again.

"Are we clear on that?" Hope said.

Her mother's eyes filled with sudden tears. She reached across the table for Hope's hand. "All I want is your happiness. You know that, don't you?"

Hope gave an inward sigh. Iris Kingsley wasn't the only expert at manipulation, she thought. Somehow her mother always knew how to diffuse Hope's anger.

"I know that," she said softly. "But I meant what I said. No matchmaking. And don't start working on Jake behind my back," she warned.

Her mother sniffed. "I wouldn't do that. But I wish you would consider what I said about moving out of that house. It's time you got away from the Kingsleys, no matter what you decide to do with the rest of your life. Mrs. Forsythe's house just went on the market, you know. She's moving to Arizona to be with her daughter. It's a little dollhouse of a place. It'd be perfect for you, Hope."

"I'm sure it's very nice, but I've already told you, I can't move out right now. Not until—"

"Until what?"

"Until things are settled," Hope replied.

"And just when do you think that will be?"

Hope shrugged. "I don't know." Soon, she hoped. She glanced at her watch. "I have to go."

"But you just got here." Her mother's face fell. "I wanted to show you the dress I got for the wedding. Of course, it doesn't compare to anything in your wardrobe," she said, almost accusingly, as she glanced at Hope's white suit. "But I did get it at Goldsmith's, in the better dresses. It was half off but it still cost an arm and a leg. I've been wondering which shoes to wear with it—"

"Sorry, Mom," Hope interrupted. "I'd love to help, but I really do have to be going."

"You're not upset with me, are you?" her mother asked anxiously as she walked Hope to the front door. "I know I can sometimes be a little blunt, but I just had to get those things off my chest. I've been so worried about you."

Hope gave her mother an affectionate hug. "I'm not upset, as long as you remember our agreement."

"I have an idea. Let's ride to the wedding together on Saturday. It'll give us a chance to talk some more."

"Sure," Hope said absently. "What time shall I pick you up?"

"The wedding's at seven. It's a candlelight service, so you'd better be here by six at least. Only, we'll take my car. That fancy rig of yours makes me nervous."

Hope just shook her head. "Whatever you say, Mom."

HER MOTHER WAS RIGHT, Hope thought. Mrs. Forsythe's house, two blocks over from the house Hope had grown up in, was absolutely perfect. It was gray brick with darker gray shutters and a concrete porch that was sheltered from the street by a trellis of wisteria.

Clay pots of impatiens and begonias, bright splashes of color against the somber background, trailed up the wide, concrete steps, and on either side of the arched opening to the porch, huge baskets of Boston fern swayed gently in the afternoon breeze.

A real-estate agent was hammering a For Sale sign into the front yard, and Hope was tempted to get out and ask the woman to show her the house.

But something held her back. Something told her the time was not yet right. Until she found out the truth about Michael Eldridge, until she set her mind at ease about Andrew, Hope knew she would never be completely free.

Chapter Four

The next morning, Jake went by Victor Northrup's plush downtown office, housed in a renovated cotton warehouse with a riverfront view, to tell Victor he would not be taking him on as a client.

Jeremy Willows, a partner at Northrup, Simmons and Fitzgerald, was in the office with Victor when Jake arrived, and Northrup quickly dismissed him. Jeremy glanced curiously at Jake before he exited the room, closing the door firmly behind him.

Northrup glared at Jake with his piercing gray eyes. "I thought you understood this was to be kept confidential."

"You wanted my answer first thing this morning," Jake said. "That's why I'm here."

Northrup waved an impatient hand, as if he couldn't be bothered with petty details. "Never mind," he said. "I'll think of something to tell Jeremy. Let's get down to business. I've put a file together that I think you might find useful. People I think you should contact—"

"Wait a minute," Jake said. "I came here to tell you that I've decided against taking you on as a client."

Northrup gazed at him in amazement. "You what?"

"I have another case," Jake said, not bothering to tell him it was the same case, different client. "I have a feeling it'll be taking most of my time."

Northrup's eyes narrowed menacingly. "Now see here, we had an agreement."

"No, we didn't," Jake said. "I told you I'd let you know my decision this morning, and I've done that."

"You're making a big mistake," Northrup warned as Jake stood to leave. "I could open a lot of doors for you, young man."

True enough, Jake thought. But the longer he was around Northrup, the more certain he became that he'd made the right decision. Northrup had a hidden agenda. A man like him always did. Jake just wasn't sure at the moment what it was, but he would find out. In due time, he would find out what Victor Northrup was up to.

"I think I'd rather open my own doors," Jake said, reaching for the knob. "But thanks anyway."

As Jake was leaving the building, Jeremy Willows caught up with him. Willows was tall and lanky, a well-groomed, unattractive man with thinning brown hair and a perpetual scowl that made him look older than his forty years.

Growing up on the Kingsley estate, Jake had often seen Willows walking around the grounds alone, never with any friends and never with Andrew. Willows had been an odd sort, even back then. The chasm between the stepbrothers had been much greater than their five-year age gap. Andrew had been outgoing and adventurous, foolhardy at times, whereas Jeremy had always been quiet and studious and prone to bouts of pouting when he didn't get his way. Which he usually did, if his mother, Pamela, had anything to say about it. According to Andrew, she doted on Jeremy while completely ignoring her stepson, except when Edward and Iris were around.

After a while, she didn't even bother to keep up the pretense. She couldn't stand Andrew, and he knew it. He'd told Jake once, when they were still friends and Andrew had still been allowed to play with Jake, that Pamela had hated Adam even more than she hated Andrew because even at the tender age of three, Adam had never been taken in by her beauty. He'd screamed bloody murder every time she came near him.

As Jake stood looking at Jeremy Willows now, the thought occurred to him that if Andrew's car crash hadn't been an accident, Jeremy and Pamela probably had the strongest motive of all for doing him in.

"What were you doing in Victor's office just now?" Jeremy asked.

"I think you'd better ask him that," Jake said.

Jeremy's eyes narrowed. "Did it have something to do with Michael Eldridge?"

Jake shrugged. "Like I said, you'd better ask Mr. Northrup that question."

"You know, of course, that my grandmother has forbidden anyone to investigate Mr. Eldridge."

Jake said nothing. He wondered if Jeremy would run tattling to Iris, and how Northrup would handle the situation if he did. But that was none of Jake's concern. He turned and started walking toward the door that would lead him to the street.

Willows fell into step beside him. "I can't think of

any other business someone like you would have with Victor Northrup.''

Jake slanted him a glance. "Maybe it's personal.''

"I don't think so. Look, all I want to know is whether or not you're working for Victor.'' They reached the door and stopped. Jeremy's permanent scowl deepened, etching crevices across his forehead. "Because if you're not, I'd like to hire you myself.''

Jake glanced at him, startled. Jeremy's gaze met his evenly. "I'd like for you to investigate Michael Eldridge for me. I'd be willing to double what Victor offered you.''

"I'm not interested,'' Jake said, stepping out into the bright sunlight. He half expected Jeremy to follow him out, but wasn't surprised when he didn't. In the old days, Jeremy had never been outwardly assertive, preferring sneakier methods instead to get what he wanted.

First Northrup, then Hope, and now Jeremy Willows wanted to hire him to investigate Michael Eldridge. Jake wondered who would be next. Pamela? Edward? It seemed everyone close to Iris Kingsley was willing to go behind her back, and Jake suspected their reasons were not all that diverse. At least where Northrup and Jeremy Willows were concerned.

If Michael Eldridge turned out to be an impostor, Jeremy stood to inherit Iris's considerable fortune.

And by protecting the Kingsley estate, Victor Northrup also protected the huge revenue—and his own generous draw—collected from the Kingsleys each year by his law firm.

Hope's motive was the only one Jake couldn't quite figure out. Was she really trying to protect Iris Kingsley from a greedy impostor, or was there another, more personal reason she was so desperate to find out about Michael Eldridge's past?

AT IRIS'S INVITATION, Michael Eldridge spent a considerable amount of time at the mansion over the next few days, mostly in Iris's company. Hope did her best to avoid him. When days had gone by and she'd managed not to run into him, she convinced herself that his resemblance to Andrew couldn't be as great as she'd initially thought. It was just the shock of his turning up so suddenly that had disturbed her.

If and when she saw the man again, she would probably wonder why she'd ever considered the possibility that he might actually be Andrew. The more time that went by, the more relieved she was that she hadn't confided her suspicions to Jake. The notion sounded crazier all the time. What had she been thinking? Dead men didn't return from the grave.

On Friday, however, Hope found she could avoid facing Michael no longer. Iris had invited him to dinner that night and informed the entire family that she would brook no excuses. Everyone was to be present.

She even suggested to Hope which outfit she would like for her to wear—pale lilac pants with a matching camisole top and a hand-painted gauzy overblouse in a pastel print. The outfit had been a gift from Andrew, and Hope started to protest, but then she thought, why not? If it made Iris happy, what could it hurt?

Hope lingered in her suite for as long as she could. By the time she finally came down, the family had already had cocktails in the library and were drifting into the dining room.

"Hope." Iris clung to Michael's arm. "You're just in time. Michael, will you escort Hope in to dinner?"

"I'd be delighted." He smiled at Hope, and her heart took a tumble inside her. For all the time she'd spent convincing herself over the past few days that her doubts and worries about Michael Eldridge were for nothing, she knew now as her gaze met his that no matter who he turned out to be, he was still a dangerous man.

And he still looked exactly like Andrew.

Reluctantly, Hope took Michael's arm, and the two of them fell in behind Iris and Edward. Jeremy and Pamela brought up the rear, a position, Hope suspected, they were both overly self-conscious about.

The table was beautifully appointed with candlelight, crystal, and china as white and delicate as snowflakes. An arrangement of white orchids in the center of the table gave a touch of the exotic to the otherwise ostentatious and somewhat somber dining room.

Iris took her place at the head of the table, with Edward on her left and Michael in the place of honor on her right. Pamela was seated next to Edward, and Hope, much to her chagrin, was wedged between Michael and Jeremy, neither of whom she would have willingly chosen to spend an entire evening with.

As the dinner progressed and the wine poured freely, Hope became aware of a subtle, cloying fragrance, a familiar scent that teased at her memory. At first she thought it was the orchids, but then it came to her with something of a shock that she was smelling Incensé, the spicy cologne Andrew had always favored.

Her heart started to pound. She couldn't tell whether the fragrance was coming from Michael or from Jeremy. She had never noticed Jeremy using any kind of cologne or after-shave at all, but Michael

Eldridge wearing the same scent Andrew had preferred was just too much of a coincidence. It *had* to be Jeremy.

She glanced in his direction and found him gazing at her quizzically, as if he'd sensed her inner distress. "Is anything wrong?" he asked, leaning toward her.

Hope shrugged. "What could be wrong?" He *was* wearing the cologne, she thought in relief. The scent had become stronger when he'd bent toward her. But in the next instant, her relief fled. Why was Jeremy wearing Andrew's fragrance?

"So what do you think of the prodigal son?" Jeremy asked. He had a wrinkle across the bridge of his nose that always made him look dour, as if his thoughts were dark and gloomy and not something Hope would want to be privy to.

She glanced at the end of the table, where Iris and Michael had their heads together like two long-lost friends. Hope had never seen Iris look so animated, so happy, and she wondered again what would happen if Michael Eldridge turned out to be an impostor. A clever, handsome, charming impostor. It struck her with something of a shock that that was exactly what Andrew had been. His outward facade had been nothing like the complex, troubled man lurking deep within.

She turned back to Jeremy. "Iris seems convinced he's her grandson. I've never seen her so happy."

If possible, Jeremy looked even gloomier. His gray eyes reminded Hope of a rain cloud, all dark and dank and full of dread. He leaned toward her again, lowering his voice so as not to be overheard. "I've thought of hiring an investigator."

Hope looked at him in surprise. She'd never known

him to go against Iris's wishes. "Who would you hire?" she asked innocently.

"I've talked to Jake McClain."

Hope tried to keep her voice neutral. "What did he say?"

Jeremy hesitated, then shrugged. "He declined. But I think he's holding out for more money. He's fallen on some pretty hard times lately."

"So I heard."

"When I think about the way he and Andrew used to strut around the grounds, both of them so damned arrogant and sure of themselves. It's ironic—isn't it? Almost funny, really, how far they both fell."

Hope said coolly, "I don't see anything funny about a man losing his life and another losing his job. Your sense of humor escapes me, Jeremy."

A faint blush colored his cheeks. "I'm sorry. I know how that must have sounded, but I didn't mean it that way. I really didn't. It's just that…when we were all kids, Jake and Andrew, especially Andrew, weren't all that kind to me."

Hope suspected that much was true. Jake and Andrew would have been two of a kind in so many ways back then—both lively and adventuresome and full of the devil. Of course, that was before Andrew had been instructed not to play with the gardener's son. That was before he'd developed his own sense of superiority. Jake had never said so, but Hope knew he'd been hurt by Andrew's rebuff. To have his friendship rejected solely because of who and what his father was would have wounded Jake's pride terribly.

But Jake's pride, Hope reminded herself, was no longer her concern. It hadn't been for a long, long time.

"I'm sorry, Hope," Jeremy said. "That really was thoughtless of me."

"It's all right," she replied, longing for the dinner to be over and done with so she could escape to her room. But before she could do that, there would be coffee in the library and more polite, stilted conversation. Jeremy would drift off to a corner, Edward would break open the brandy, and Pamela's shrill laughter would become as nerve-racking as fingernails scraping a chalkboard.

But no one, including Hope, would dare leave until Iris retired for the night. In the ten years Hope had been married to Andrew, the evenings at the Kingsley mansion had not varied one iota. Andrew and Iris were the only ones who had ever remotely enjoyed themselves. After his death, Iris had continued the nightly ritual, but she would linger no longer than half an hour or so before calling it a night.

Tonight, however, as Hope watched Michael escort Iris back into the library, she knew a reprieve would be a long time in coming. Iris would not be anxious to relinquish Michael's company. The evening would wear on forever.

"That's a beautiful outfit, Hope."

Startled, she found herself face-to-face with Michael Eldridge. He had finally left Iris's side and was standing directly in front of Hope, too close for comfort. She fought the urge to step back from him.

"Thank you," she murmured.

His dark blue eyes deepened approvingly as his gaze slipped over her. "That's exactly the color I would have chosen for you myself."

Hope didn't like the note of familiarity in his tone.

Nor did she like the way he looked at her with proprietary eyes. Andrew's eyes.

She shivered. The French doors were open to the April night, and a breeze drifted through the room, stirring the scent of jonquils and narcissus, and tinkling the teardrop crystals of the Waterford chandelier.

"Why do I get the impression," Michael said softly, "that I make you uncomfortable?"

Because you do, Hope thought. Instead she said, "Maybe it's your imagination."

One dark brow cocked. So like Andrew. "Is it?"

The cloying scent of Andrew's cologne drifted to her again, and Hope realized she must have been mistaken earlier. It hadn't been Jeremy wearing Incensé. It was Michael Eldridge. And the coincidence, on top of everything else, was almost too stunning to bear.

He leaned toward her and the fragrance filled her senses. Sparked her fear. "Do I look that much like him, Hope? Is that why you're afraid to be alone with me?"

"I'm not," she protested, her hand inching to her throat. The walls of the library felt as if they were closing in on her. Hope wanted nothing more than to get away from this man, to get away from this house, to get away from her past. But she stood rooted to the spot by some horrible fascination, by some dreaded premonition of events yet to unfold.

"You do look like Andrew," she finally admitted. "Very much."

"Is that painful for you?" His gaze intensified. "It must be, if you were in love with him."

The last was said almost in accusation. Hope drew

herself up, bristling at his tone. "My marriage is really none of your concern."

He looked immediately contrite. "Was I prying? I'm sorry. I didn't mean to. It's just that I'm curious about you. I'm curious about everyone." He turned to sweep the room with a brief glance. "Jeremy, Pamela, Edward. And dear, sweet Iris."

Hope thought his words sounded facetious, but his eyes held no trace of guile. "Those are adjectives not usually associated with Iris Kingsley," she said.

"Why not? She's a pussycat."

"To you, maybe." And to Andrew. But to everyone else she could be a merciless tyrant, although Hope had always managed to stay in her good graces. Iris had once told her that she'd felt an immediate bond with Hope the moment Andrew had brought her home. Hope reminded Iris of herself when she was young, she'd said wistfully, and Hope had been flattered. What twenty-two-year-old wouldn't be? A charming, sophisticated, worldly woman like Iris Kingsley comparing herself to a kindergarten teacher who'd never traveled farther from home than Nashville.

Michael turned back to Hope, drawing her attention away from Iris. "You fascinate me more than anyone, though."

Hope tried to keep her tone casual. "Why?"

He shrugged. "The others are so easy to read. Jeremy, with his inferiority complex and resentment, Pamela with her greed and ambition, and Edward with his spent mind and self-destructive demons. Even Iris with her thirst for power and her need to control holds no mystery for me. But you're different. I can't quite figure you out."

"There's nothing to figure out."

"That's not true. For instance, why are you still living in this house? Your husband's been dead for over five months."

"It's my home," Hope replied, trying not to sound defensive. After all, she didn't owe Michael Eldridge any explanations. She didn't have to justify herself to him just because he looked like Andrew.

"I don't think so," Michael said. "I don't think this is your home. In fact, most of the time you remind me of a caged bird waiting for the chance to escape." His gaze darkened slightly. "You never liked it here, did you?"

His tone sent a chill up Hope's spine. His insight made her shiver with dread. "Who are you?" she whispered.

He pretended not to hear her at first, then he smiled slowly, and the chill deepened around Hope's heart. "You know who I am, Hope. My name is Michael Eldridge...at least for the time being."

A LITTLE WHILE LATER, Michael went to kiss Iris's cheek and bid her good-night. The whole room seemed to breathe a collective sigh of relief when he left. Everyone except Iris, who, all of a sudden, looked fragile and delicate and extremely vulnerable.

As Hope had anticipated, Jeremy had grown more withdrawn as the evening wore on, Pamela's laughter had become more false, and Edward was now working on his fourth brandy. He didn't appear to notice as his mother struggled to her feet and summoned Hope to help her upstairs.

Iris's steps were even slower than usual as they ascended the curved marble stairway with its silk runner and carved mahogany banister. She clung to Hope's arm for support, and in spite of herself, Hope couldn't help remembering her mother's words. *"You may not see her manipulations, but I certainly do."*

Was Iris's vulnerability tonight a subtle form of manipulation? Hope wondered, then was immediately ashamed of her thoughts. The woman was eighty-five years old. She had a right to succumb to frailty now and again.

Inside the green and gold suite, Iris sat down on a gold brocade chair and motioned Hope to the settee across from her.

"We haven't had a chance to talk much lately," she said. "I've hardly seen you at all in the last few days."

"I've been pretty busy," Hope told her.

"So I've heard. You've been substitute teaching at Claymore."

"For a couple of days, yes."

Iris's eyes grew wistful. "I was a teacher, too, when I met Edward's father. I'm sure I've told you the story many times. We have so much in common, you and I. I've always thought so. It means so much to me to have you here, my dear. I hope you know that."

"You've always made me feel welcome," Hope said truthfully.

Iris sighed. "Wasn't it wonderful to have Michael with us this evening?"

"I'm glad you had a good time."

Iris's dark blue gaze met Hope's. "I saw the two of you talking."

Hope shrugged. "We were just getting acquainted." She had no intention of telling Iris how disturbed she was by her conversation with Michael Eldridge, or how even more convinced she was now that he was a dangerous man. Iris wouldn't believe her anyway. Not without proof.

"I probably shouldn't say this," Iris began hesitantly. "Andrew's only been gone from us for five months, but…" She leaned toward Hope. "I think Michael is quite taken with you."

Hope gazed at Iris in astonishment. Just after Andrew's death, Iris had made it clear to Hope that she expected the two of them to be in mourning for a long time to come. Now, here she was suggesting…acting as if…

"I'm sure you're mistaken," Hope murmured uncomfortably.

"Perhaps," Iris mused. She fell silent for a moment, then said, "For years now the thing I desired most in this world was for you and Andrew to produce a child together, a great-grandson who would carry on the Kingsley name. After Andrew died, I thought that was lost to me forever, but now that Michael has entered our lives…"

She trailed off as Hope stared at her in horror. *Don't,* she thought. *Please, don't even think such a thing.*

Surely she'd misconstrued Iris's meaning. Surely Iris wasn't suggesting that Hope and Michael Eldridge…

"I'm so tired tonight," Iris said weakly. Her hand fluttered to her heart. "I have so little strength these days. Perhaps I should turn in." She smiled as Hope took her cue and stood to leave. "Good night, my dear. I hope you have pleasant dreams."

There wasn't much chance of that, Hope thought,

as she let herself out of Iris's room. She started toward her own room in a different wing of the house, then suddenly reversed her steps and headed for the stairway. The prospect of spending a sleepless night in the suite she'd shared with Andrew had even less appeal than usual. As she descended the stairs, she decided to take a walk in the garden to try and clear her head.

As she passed the library, the murmur of voices drew her attention for a moment. Hope assumed everyone had retired when Iris did, but through the open double doors, she could see Edward asleep in a wing chair near the fireplace, his head thrown back, his jaw slack, his mouth open. An empty brandy snifter had fallen from his hand and was lying on the priceless Persian rug at his feet.

Hope wondered for a moment if she should go in and try to wake him, help him to bed, but Pamela's disgusted voice stopped her. "Leave him. He'll stumble upstairs eventually. God help me."

"Why do you put up with this, Mother?" Jeremy demanded.

"You know why," Pamela said wearily. "We've been all through this. It won't be for much longer."

Hope backed away from the library, not wanting to be caught eavesdropping. But a part of her wondered if she should have stayed. Something about that conversation disturbed her. It was as if Pamela and Jeremy were plotting something. As if they had already put some grand scheme into motion.

Letting herself out one of the French doors in the drawing room that faced the rear gardens, Hope slipped into the darkness, shivering a bit in the April breeze. She wished she'd grabbed a sweater before coming out.

Skirting the pool, she headed for the deeper recesses of the garden, where the giant topiary sculptures cast menacing shadows in the moonlight. The night wind stirred the fragrance of spring flowers—jonquils, hyacinths and wisteria. The heavenly aroma settled over the garden like a gossamer veil, but underneath was a more subtle fragrance, a scent that was darker and deeper than the flowers. Mysterious and yet familiar.

Incensé, Hope realized with a shudder of dread.

She turned at the sound of rustling leaves behind her. Someone was out there. Someone was watching her. Hope's heart started to pound in fear.

SHE STOOD AS STILL AS a statue. In the moonlight, her complexion looked as smooth and flawless as marble, her beauty timeless and mysterious. Jake stood staring at her for a long moment before stepping from the shadows to confront her.

Her hand flew to her throat when she saw him. "Jake!" she said breathlessly. "You startled me."

There was an odd note of relief in her voice that should have flattered him, but didn't. Possibly because he'd seen her stiffen in fear a split second before she'd recognized him. Something had spooked her this evening, and Jake wanted to know what.

"You're out late." He stepped into the moonlight beside her and saw that she was trembling. "Are you all right?"

She wore her hair up, but a few soft strands curled about her face. She pushed them back with a hand that didn't look quite steady. "Of course," she said.

"I just came out for a walk before bedtime. You startled me, that's all."

"So you said." The silky fabric of her blouse floated in the breeze, as light and airy as a whisper, making her seem hardly more than an illusion. Jake turned to the mansion. "He was there tonight, wasn't he?"

Hope moved beside him, in a tiny, abrupt gesture that betrayed her nerves. "Yes."

"How did it go?"

For a moment, she said nothing. Jake turned to gaze down at her in the pale light. Her profile made him catch his breath. Then she said, "Iris is more convinced than ever that he's...her grandson."

"That he's Adam Kingsley."

A slight hesitation, then, "Yes," she said in almost a whisper. She turned to gaze up at him. The darkness deepened the violet of her eyes. Or was it something else? "What have you found out about him so far?"

Jake shrugged. "The preliminary stuff has all checked out—social-security number, driver's license, school and employment records. There is a Michael Eldridge, no question."

"What will you do next?"

"Go down to Houston," Jake said. "Flash his picture around. Talk to his friends, business associates, try to get a lead on some of the foster homes he stayed in."

"How did you get a picture of him?" Hope asked in surprise.

Jake grinned. "Do you really want to know?"

"If Iris knew you were lurking around the grounds with a camera, she'd have all our heads," Hope said worriedly. "Your father's included."

"She won't find out. I'm good at what I do, Hope. Trust me."

Her gaze met his. She drew a long, trembling breath that did things to Jake—things he wanted to deny. "I do trust you," she said softly. "That's why I came to you for help."

Her eyes looked like violet mist in the sterling light, her lips like the dewy petals of a rose. Soft and sweet. Irresistible.

The breeze stirred the curls at her neck, drawing Jake's gaze to the creamy skin at her throat. And lower, to the hint of cleavage above her camisole top. He wanted to kiss her, he realized. Really kiss her. But the question was, would she let him? Would she resist or succumb? Slap his face or kiss him back?

It was a gamble, Jake decided, no matter how you looked at it.

As if reading his thoughts, Hope took a little half-step away from him, but Jake reached out to cup the nape of her neck—so soft and alluring—and gently pull her back to him.

"Jake, no," she whispered.

"Why not?"

"The past is over," she said with an edge of desperation. "We both agreed."

"I'm not thinking of the past," he said. "I'm firmly grounded in the here and now. And I want to kiss you, Hope. You have no idea how badly."

"But—" Her voice sounded shaky, as if she didn't quite trust her resistance. Jake pressed his advantage, felt her yield ever so slightly. "It'll only confuse things," she said. "Mess everything up."

"No, it won't. How could it? We're older now. Smarter. We can handle this. Besides," he said, "maybe it'll get it out of our systems. We can stop wondering if there's anything left between us."

"Maybe I don't want to know," she said softly, almost sadly. "Maybe it would hurt too much to know." But she didn't back away from him this time, and Jake knew that in spite of what she'd said, a part of her needed to know. Once and for all. No matter what the consequences.

He lifted his other hand to her shoulder and pulled her to him. This time she didn't resist. This time she came willingly into his arms. He held her for a moment, gazing down at her in the moonlight. Then he bent to feather a kiss on her forehead, down her jawline, and finally, when he could deny himself no longer, he touched his mouth to hers.

Her lips trembled beneath his. Her eyes drifted closed and for a moment, the world stopped and time stood still. Nothing existed in the universe but the two of them, a man and a woman. Lovers reunited in this garden of Eden. This paradise of moonlight and memories.

When he would have deepened the kiss, Jake held back. The passion was there, yes, but...that could wait. This was something different. Something special. Something so fragile he knew it would easily shatter if he wasn't careful.

A deep sadness filled him for all the lost years. For all the wasted love. For all that could have been theirs.

He pulled back and stared down at her. Hope's eyes shimmered in the moonlight. A tear rolled down her cheek, and Jake felt something powerful stir inside him—an emotion he couldn't quite bring himself to name.

He thumbed the tear away and whispered to her in the darkness. "I know," he said. "I know."

Chapter Five

The Club Mystique was a dingy, hole-in-the-wall nightclub that had once seen better days as a gas station. Located on a two-lane state highway between Memphis and Shepherd, it seemed an unlikely place for someone like Andrew Kingsley to frequent. But Jake had discovered after Andrew's wreck that he had been a regular there. The bartender, a big, beefy ex-marine named Fred, who had a barbed-wire tattoo around his left wrist, had remembered Andrew well.

He remembered Jake, too, and scowled when Jake sat down at the bar. "Sergeant McClain, isn't it?"

Jake didn't bother to inform the man that he was no longer with the Memphis PD. Instead he ordered a Michelob.

The bartender slid the icy bottle across the bar to Jake. "What brings you out this way again—business or pleasure?"

Jake shrugged. "A little of both, maybe." Truth was, he wasn't sure what the hell he was doing here. Why he'd felt compelled to visit Andrew Kingsley's watering hole again. Why he couldn't let Hope's dead husband rest in peace. He glanced around. "Nice place you got here. I couldn't stay away."

Fred sneered. "Yeah, right."

Jake wondered if the reason Andrew had been attracted to this place was because he'd had a need to see how the other half lived. But Andrew had never been one of the guilty rich, needing to atone for his wealth. He'd always loved what money could buy, and had never made any bones about it.

A more likely rationale for his hanging out here was the fact that Simon Pratt's walled compound was only a few miles down the road. Had he been on his way to see Pratt the night he died?

Jake slid a twenty toward Fred to pay for his beer. "Keep the change."

The bartender slipped the bill into his shirt pocket. "Much obliged," he said. "Now what do you want?"

Jake shrugged. "I thought maybe you'd remembered something else about the night Andrew Kingsley cracked up his car. Maybe something about the woman he was with that night."

Fred scowled. "Hell, that was months ago. My memory ain't what it used to be."

Jake took another twenty from his wallet and laid it on the counter. When the bartender started to reach for it, Jake set his beer bottle on top of it. "You said she was driving Kingsley's car when they left the parking lot. You still sure about that?"

Fred shrugged his huge shoulders. "No reason not to be sure. I saw them with my own two eyes."

"What did she look like?"

The bartender folded his arms and glared at Jake. "Didn't you write any of this stuff down? What the hell kind of cop are you?"

"Just humor me, okay?" He removed the bottle from the twenty and Fred grabbed it.

"Like I said, she was blond, about so high." He measured the air with his hand. "And stacked. I mean really built. But she didn't look cheap like most of the chicks who come in here. She was, you know, classy looking. Like her." His gaze strayed beyond Jake's left shoulder.

Jake turned and then did a double take. Hope stood just inside the doorway, gazing around the shabby bar as if it were an alien spacecraft. A wolf whistle sounded from somewhere in the back, and for a moment, she looked as if she might turn and bolt. Then her gaze lit on Jake and surprise flashed across her features. She started toward him.

How had she found this place? Jake wondered. And what the hell was she doing here?

What am I doing here? Hope thought desperately. Her face flushed as someone called, "Hey, baby. Buy you a drink?" and someone else made a loud kissing sound.

She would have turned and fled then and there if she hadn't seen Jake at the bar. Relief washed over her, but she resisted the urge to throw herself into his arms. After last night, he might get the wrong idea, and who could blame him? She'd let him kiss her, after all. She'd let him kiss her, and then, like an idiot, she'd cried and she wasn't even sure why. She never cried.

Liar, a little voice whispered inside her. Deep down, she knew exactly why Jake's kiss had moved her so much. Even after ten years of self-denial, even after a decade of telling herself she and Jake might not have made it anyway, that one kiss had reminded Hope of how deep their feelings had once run. That one kiss had torn away her defenses, bared her soul, and shown her what she had lost ten years ago. What she had so carelessly thrown away.

Jake stood as she approached the bar and drew her down on the barstool beside him. "What are you doing here?"

"I might ask you the same thing," she replied, then glanced at the bartender. "A glass of white wine, please."

The bartender nodded toward Jake. "That's just what *she* asked for that night."

Hope turned to Jake. "She, who?"

Jake's gaze, usually so direct, faltered a bit. Then he shrugged. "The woman Andrew was with the night he died."

"Oh." Hope turned back to the bar as a napkin and a glass of wine were placed in front of her. She picked up the glass and took a sip, willing her hand to remain steady.

This was nothing new, she reminded herself. There had always been rumors of Andrew's womanizing, but Hope had never believed them. He liked to flirt. She knew that. He also craved attention. But she'd also known that Andrew had loved her, in his own way. He had his vices—the fast cars, the gambling, living life on the edge. But in spite of everything, she'd never believed he'd been unfaithful to her—until this very moment.

She tried to decide how she felt about that. How she felt about Jake's knowing. Did that make her seem less of a woman to him?

The bartender snapped his fingers. "Say, I do remember something else about the blonde, after all. Besides the white wine, I mean. Your friend here must have knocked something loose in my memory.''

"What?''

"Her name was Carol. I remember Kingsley saying something like, 'Carol needs a drink.' Yeah, Carol.'' The bartender nodded in satisfaction. "I never told you that, did I?''

"No, you didn't,'' Jake said. "And you just remembered it out of the blue like that?''

Fred shrugged. "So sue me.''

"How long did they talk?'' Hope asked. She could feel Jake's eyes on her and wondered what he was thinking.

The bartender glanced at Jake, who shrugged, giving him the go-ahead to talk freely in front of Hope.

"Twenty minutes. Half an hour, maybe.''

"And you'd never seen them together before?'' Hope asked.

"Like I said, I never saw her before that night. She wasn't the type of woman who comes to a place like this. Neither are you, for that matter.'' He gave Hope an approving once-over that made her distinctly uncomfortable. "You a cop, too?''

She glanced at Jake. A faint smile touched his lips. "Jake and I are collaborating on a case.''

"That so?''

"Yeah,'' Jake said. "That's so. Has my friend here jogged anything else loose in your memory?''

"Not a thing. I've told you everything I know.''

Hope opened her purse, but the bartender held up his hand. "It's on the house,'' he said, giving her a wink. "A babe like you adds a little class to the joint. Know what I mean?''

"WHY DID YOU COME HERE?" Jake asked her again as they left the bar together.

Hope shrugged. "I've been doing a lot of thinking lately. About Andrew. About the questions you asked after he died. The suspicions you had about him. I guess I came here to see if I could get some answers."

"You didn't want answers to those questions before," he reminded her. "You didn't believe my suspicions."

She glanced up at him. A shadow flickered across her face. "I didn't *want* to believe them. There's a difference."

"So what's changed, Hope?" The kiss they'd shared last night? A part of Jake wanted to believe she'd been as profoundly affected as he, but another part of him—the realistic part—told him that Hope's attitude probably had very little to do with him. Something was going on inside the Kingsley mansion. Inside Hope's head. He wished to hell she would level with him.

She shrugged. "I'm not sure what's changed. I just know I need some answers." She hesitated, then added, "Why are you here, Jake? Why can't *you* put Andrew's death to rest?"

"I wish to hell I knew." But maybe he did know, Jake thought. Maybe one of the reasons was standing right in front of him. "I guess I just don't like loose ends. I like everything wrapped up and tied with a neat little bow."

Hope gave him an ironic glance. "Life's rarely that simple, is it?"

"No, but I keep hoping."

She fell silent, as if thinking about what he'd said.

Then, after a moment, she glanced up at him. "Show me where Andrew's car was parked that night."

Jake led her across the cracked pavement, to a space near the back of the lot.

She glanced around, then rested her hands on her hips. "How could the bartender see his car all the way over here? How could he be so positive the woman left with Andrew?"

She was still trying to find a more desirable explanation than the obvious, Jake realized. "The bartender doubles as a bouncer. He had to throw somebody out just as Andrew and the blonde were leaving. He saw them walk over to Andrew's car, talk for a moment, then the woman climbed in behind the wheel, and they took off."

"But the Shepherd police said Andrew was driving. He was alone in the car when it crashed. And besides," Hope said, "Andrew would never have willingly let someone else drive his Porsche, no matter how attractive she was. He loved that car."

"Maybe he wasn't in any condition to drive," Jake suggested.

"You mean because he'd had too much to drink?"

"The bartender said it looked to him as if the woman was having to help Andrew to the car."

"That still doesn't ring true," Hope mused. "He would have called a cab or Iris's driver to come pick him up if he'd had too much to drink. He'd done it before. It wasn't like Andrew to trust his car to a stranger."

Jake said nothing. What was there to say? No matter what she claimed to the contrary, Hope still didn't want to know the truth about Andrew. She still remained loyal to the bitter end. Jake wondered if he admired that trait or despised it.

"I know what you're thinking," she said. "That I'm still defending Andrew as I did the night you came to question me after he died. But it's not like that anymore."

"You accused me of trying to darken his memory," Jake reminded her. "Out of revenge."

She glanced away, rubbing one temple with her fingertips. "I know. But it was easier to lash out at you than to face my own guilt."

"What did you have to feel guilty about?"

Her hand dropped to her side, but she still didn't look at him. For a long moment, she said nothing.

"Hope," Jake prompted. "What were you talking about?"

She closed her eyes briefly. "I asked Andrew for a divorce the night he died. We had a terrible fight before he left the house. If he had too much to drink that night, it was because of me, because of the terrible things I said to him. Because of what I wished..." Her voice, hollow and distant, trailed away.

A car pulling into the lot caught her in its headlights for a second, and Jake saw her wince, as if the light revealed too much. As if she wanted to remain hiding in the dark.

Jake's own insides twisted in turmoil. Hope had wanted a divorce. The word seemed to echo in the darkness, but Jake's first rush of elation fell as flat as uncorked champagne. In some ways a divorce would have been more final, he thought. Andrew's death, with all its unanswered questions, with all its emotional baggage, would now always come between them.

"Andrew was a grown man," he said. "You didn't force him to drink too much that night. You didn't force him to pick up a strange woman in a seedy bar. And you're not responsible for what happened to him later."

"I guess that's why I'm here," she said. "I guess I'm looking for a reprieve. Some sort of closure." At last she turned to face him. "Tell me about that night, Jake. Tell me what you think happened."

"I don't know that much," he said, running a hand through his hair. "There've been too many damned doors slammed in my face to find out much of anything. But I'm pretty sure the woman, or someone, was with Andrew when his car crashed because the passenger side of the windshield was cracked, like someone had been thrown up against it. The blonde either left the scene or was removed before the police ever arrived, and then Andrew's body was placed near the driver's side, to make it look as if he'd been alone in the car."

"But why?"

Jake shrugged again. "The obvious reason would be to salvage his reputation."

"Which means you think Iris was behind it." Hope fingered the top button of her sweater. "But how could she have found out about the crash so quickly?"

"She couldn't unless she was having someone follow Andrew. Or unless the Shepherd police called her before they reported the accident."

"Why would they do that?"

"Because I think she had them bought and paid

for. At least some of them. I think she made sure she had the local authorities in her pocket the moment I started investigating Andrew's connection to Simon Pratt."

"Do you have any evidence of her involvement?" Hope asked.

"Not really," Jake admitted. "But it seemed strange to me that an autopsy wasn't performed on Andrew's body to determine the exact cause of death."

Hope stared at him in shock. "What do you mean, there wasn't an autopsy? Of course there was."

"I know for a fact there wasn't," Jake told her.

"But I was told...or maybe I just assumed..." In the filtered light from the streetlamps, Hope's face took on a strange expression.

"Andrew was DOA at Shepherd Memorial Hospital. The local authorities determined there was no cause for an autopsy. Death was accidental. One of the residents had already drawn blood for the toxicology screen, but the results were never released."

"I knew about that," Hope said. "When Iris and I arrived at the hospital that night, I heard one of the doctors say blood samples had been taken and turned over to the police lab. I guess from that I just assumed there'd been an autopsy. I didn't think much about it until later, when Michael Eldridge showed up. I remembered then that the police had a sample of Andrew's blood that could be used for the DNA testing."

"I'm surprised Iris didn't have the samples destroyed," Jake said. "Although I guess suppressing the report was all that was necessary."

"Because he'd been drinking, you mean."

"Exactly. If he didn't leave the bar with that woman, then he was DUI. Either way, Iris would have wanted to clean up his mess. She's always been obsessed with maintaining the Kingsley name."

"Yes, I know," Hope said. Another shadow flashed across her face. "I just hadn't realized how far she might be willing to go."

Jake looked at her in surprise. "I can't believe you just said that. You've always defended Iris Kingsley."

Hope glanced away. "Maybe I still should be defending her," she said with a shrug. "We don't have any proof that she did any of the things you think she did."

"True," Jake conceded. "But someone did tamper with the accident scene. Someone did buy off the Shepherd police so that no autopsy was performed. If Iris didn't do it to protect Andrew's reputation, then I can only conclude someone else with a more sinister purpose was behind it."

"Someone like Simon Pratt?" Her quickness surprised him.

"That thought has crossed my mind," he agreed.

"At the time of Andrew's death, you alluded to some sort of connection between him and Pratt. What did you think you had on him, Jake?"

"Andrew owed Pratt a lot of money. One way or another, Pratt always collects."

"So…you think he had something to do with the car crash?" Hope asked.

"I think it's a possibility, yes," Jake said grimly. "What I can't figure out is where the woman comes in."

"Maybe she doesn't," Hope said. "Maybe her leaving the bar with Andrew was just…coincidental."

"Maybe," Jake said. But he'd been a cop for too long to chalk anything up to chance.

"How far is the crash site from here?" Hope asked.

"Couple of miles."

"Will you take me there?"

Jake stared down at her in the darkness. "Haven't you been out there before?"

She shook her head. "No. I didn't want to before, but now I need to see where it happened… It's something I have to do."

Jake shrugged. "All right. If that's what you want."

But as much as he wanted to buy her story about guilt and reprieves and looking for closure, he didn't think that was her real reason for coming here tonight. The events surrounding Andrew's death were shrouded in mystery, and now Hope's behavior was yet another.

THE ROAD WAS DESERTED as they pulled onto the highway and headed east, toward Shepherd. A half mile or so from town, Jake pulled his Blazer to the side of the road and parked. Hope looked out her window. A steep embankment led down to a meadow of scrawny shrubs and brambles, and to a thick woods beyond. A light fog had settled knee-high over the countryside, giving the night a strange, surreal ambience. A shiver of fear crept up Hope's spine. Did she really want to do this?

"You sure about this?" Jake asked.

She glanced at him and nodded.

They got out of the truck, and Jake came around

to take her arm. He had a flashlight, but the beam scarcely penetrated the fog.

"The car went off the road about here," he said. "In the daylight, you can still see the skid marks."

Hope followed the flashlight beam with her eyes, trying to imagine what Andrew's last few moments had been like. Had he been alone? Had he been afraid? Had he known what was about to happen to him?

Had he even been in that car?

Hope shivered again as Jake led her down the embankment. Mist curled like smoke around their legs as they walked through the tall grass toward the trees.

Jake played the flashlight beam along the trunk of a massive red oak. Even in the darkness and fog, Hope could see the deep scars in the bark where Andrew's Porsche had smashed into it, and a faint trail of red paint. Andrew had always been partial to red cars.

"I had a contact in the sheriff's department in Shepherd who notified me as soon as they got the call about the wreck. I drove out here as fast as I could, but the ambulance had already left with Andrew," Jake said.

"What made you think his body had been moved?" Hope asked, her gaze still on the scarred tree.

"Besides the cracked windshield, there were marks on the ground around the car, like something had been dragged from one side to the other. The Shepherd police had trampled all over the area, and on top of that, it had started to rain. I didn't think much about it at first, but then I got to thinking. From the little I could learn at the hospital, Andrew had suffered a severe head trauma, which would be consistent with the cracked windshield. Also, the Shepherd police told me that the driver's door was flung open and Andrew's body was lying outside. If he'd been wearing his seat belt, he wouldn't have been thrown out of the car like that."

"Which is why, when you came to see me later, you asked me if Andrew always wore his seat belt," Hope said.

"And you said, as far as you knew, he always did."

"It was kind of a thing with him," she explained. "He had a friend who was paralyzed in a car crash a few years ago because he wasn't wearing his seat belt. The man's wife and child were killed. It affected Andrew deeply. He loved to drive fast, but he didn't take unnecessary risks. He wouldn't have been driving without wearing his seat belt, and he wouldn't have been driving while intoxicated."

Jake watched her walk away from the tree and stand for a moment, gazing at the shrouded countryside. She had no way of knowing, of course, but she stood near the spot where Andrew's body had been found. Jake wondered if she sensed it somehow, because even in the darkness he could see her shiver.

He walked over to her. "Like I said. There're a lot of unanswered questions about Andrew's death. Questions that may never be answered."

"But you haven't given up, have you?" Hope asked quietly. "That's why you were at the bar tonight. That's why you brought me out here."

"I brought you out here because you asked me to," Jake told her. "And now that I have, tell me something, Hope. Did you get what you came for?"

She folded her arms around her middle, huddling inside her pink sweater. "I'm not sure. I guess I thought if I saw the place, experienced it for myself, I'd somehow *know*...."

"Know what?"

She turned to him. He couldn't see her expression in the dark, but he could hear the desperation in her voice. Or was it fear? "Did you see him that night, Jake?"

It took him a moment to get her meaning. Then, "You mean Andrew? You mean...afterward?" When she nodded, he said, "I told you, the ambulance had already taken him away when I got here."

"I know, but what about at the hospital? Or the morgue?" The last word was said in almost a whisper.

Jake stared down at her in confusion. "What's going on here, Hope?"

"Nothing," she replied, but her tone was far from convincing. "I just want to know if you saw him."

Jake shook his head, still puzzled by the question. "No. I didn't see him. His death was ruled accidental by the coroner, and at any rate, I had no jurisdiction here. There was no reason for them to let me see him."

She gazed up at the sky, her profile an enigma in the hazy light from the moon. "I didn't see him, either. Did you know that? I was legally the next of kin, but they wouldn't let me see him, and Iris agreed. She had Victor Northrup identify the body. The doctor at the hospital and then later the Shepherd police all delicately informed me that it would be too traumatic for me to see Andrew's body. The crash had—done things to him, they said."

"That's entirely possible," Jake said. "However, there wasn't that much blood at the scene."

His response seemed to send another shiver scuttling through Hope. He saw her shudder and clutch her arms more tightly around her middle. Jake touched his hand to her arm and she jumped.

"Hope," he said. "What's going on? Why all these morbid questions?"

She shook her head. "It's crazy," she whispered. "You wouldn't believe me if I told you."

"Try me." He placed his hands on her arms and turned her to face him. Mist swirled around them, wrapping them in a cocoon of damp softness. But far from being a comfort, it seemed to heighten the strangeness of the night.

Somewhere in the distance, a dog howled and the hair on the back of Jake's neck prickled with awareness. *Damn,* he thought. The place was getting to him. He had the strongest notion that if he looked over his shoulder, he might see Andrew walking out of the woods toward them.

"Come on," he said. "Let's get out of here."

"Wait," Hope said. "Just give me a minute more. I need to—"

Her words were cut off by a motion from Jake. He lifted his finger to his lips, commanding silence. Maybe it was his imagination, but he thought he heard something in the woods.

Beside him, Hope stiffened in fear. Her gaze followed his, to the patch of darkness just off to their right. Silently, Jake drew his gun. He gestured for Hope to stay put as he moved in front of her and started walking toward the shadows.

Chapter Six

Out of the corner of her eye, Hope saw something move in the darkness beside her. She had only the briefest impression of tallness, of broad shoulders tapering to a narrow waist and lean hips, as the man rushed out of the shadows toward her. Before she could utter a sound, his arm came around her neck and he aimed a gun at her temple.

Hope gasped, her heart thundering in her ears. As if from a distance, she heard a voice she didn't recognize yell, "Drop it!" to Jake. Relief flooded over her, and then in the next instant, Hope thought what an idiot she was. A man held a gun to her head, and her strongest emotion was one of relief, because he was a stranger. Because he wasn't Andrew.

She saw Jake edge slowly toward them in the darkness. The arm around her throat tightened. She could feel the cool metal of the gun barrel against her skin. "I said, drop it."

Jake hesitated for just a split second, then tossed his gun to the ground.

"Now kick it over here," the man ordered.

Again Jake complied. The man released Hope and gave her a shove with the gun. "Pick it up."

She bent to retrieve the gun. The moment she had it in her hand, Hope had the urge to turn and fire, but she knew the man would shoot her dead before she ever got off the first shot, let alone aimed in the darkness.

She straightened and handed him the weapon. He took it and slipped it into his pocket, then with the barrel of his own gun, motioned Jake over. When Jake stood beside Hope, the man moved around behind them. "Start walking," he ordered. "Toward the highway."

They headed through the meadow of brambles toward the road. Jake asked cautiously, "What's the crime?"

"Trespassing. You got a problem with that, take it up with Mr. Pratt."

"Pratt?" Jake glanced over his shoulder. His movements were very slow and deliberate, Hope noticed. He wasn't taking any chances, probably because of her. "What's he got to do with this?"

"This is his property," the man told them.

"Since when?"

"Since this morning. Now get moving."

Jake took Hope's elbow and they scrambled up the embankment together. When they reached the road, the man took Hope's arm and drew her away from Jake. Walking toward Jake's truck, the man told Jake to drive.

His hand on her arm made Hope cringe. It was all she could do not to struggle. She watched Jake crawl behind the wheel, then, after a nudge of the gun, she climbed into the back and the man got in beside her.

Jake started the engine, and in the light from the dash, she saw their captor for the first time. As she'd thought, he was tall and muscular, and had dark blond hair and a thick mustache. He was dressed in a black double-breasted suit with a black shirt underneath. Obviously he hadn't been dressed to go tramping about in the woods, so he must have followed them from the bar.

He was handsome in a slick kind of way, but the look he gave Hope made her nervous. Made her feel as though she needed to wash her hands.

Over his shoulder Jake asked, "Which way?"

"Straight ahead, then make a right. I'll tell you when."

Jake pulled onto the road. "You must be new." His gaze met Hope's in the rearview mirror. "I thought I knew all of Pratt's thugs, but I don't remember you."

"Shut up," the man said. "And keep driving."

They all fell silent. Hope's gaze met Jake's in the mirror again, and he nodded ever so slightly, as if trying to reassure her. A few miles up the road, the man tapped on the window with the gun barrel. "Turn here."

Jake swung off the road onto what seemed hardly more than a dirt trail through the woods. They bumped over potholes and metal cattle guards for another mile or so until suddenly they hit pavement. Jake pulled the truck to a stop at a metal gate set into a ten-foot-high brick wall. The man beside Hope removed a small transmitter from his pocket, touched a button, and the metal gates slid apart. Jake drove through.

All along the winding drive, Hope noticed tiny red lights glowing intermittently from the trees. Surveillance cameras, she guessed, and then, as they neared the house, the woods thinned and she saw guards with automatic weapons and Doberman pinschers on leashes patrolling the property. Simon Pratt was taking no chances, either.

Jake drew up in front of the house, a huge Tudor-style mansion that reminded Hope of the Kingsley estate, and killed the engine. "What now?"

"Get out," the man said. He opened the door and slid out, then motioned for Hope to do the same. She went to stand beside Jake and he took her hand, gently squeezing her fingers in encouragement. He would get them out of this mess, he silently communicated. Somehow.

They walked up the steps to the front door, and once inside the massive foyer, the man behind them relinquished Jake's gun to the guard at the door. "Search them," he commanded.

The guard frisked Jake roughly, searching for hidden weapons. When he started to do the same to Hope, Jake shoved him away. Instantly two other guards were on the scene. They both grabbed Jake and held him while Hope was subjected to a search.

Her face flaming, Hope closed her eyes as the man's hands moved over her. Then it was done, and she and Jake were led down a long corridor to a set of polished mahogany doors with gold handles. The man with the gun touched another button on his transmitter, and one of the doors swung silently inward.

Jake and Hope stepped inside the room. It was a library, again not unlike the one at the Kingsley mansion. Floor-to-ceiling windows adorned one wall while bookshelves occupied the two end walls. Deep leather chairs were artfully arranged around a marble fireplace, and the hardwood floor was softened by huge Oriental rugs. A flamboyant Matisse hung over the mantel, looking incongruous in the otherwise-somber room.

A man in a maroon silk robe sat behind a massive carved desk near the windows. He looked to be in his late sixties, with dark gray hair and bags under his eyes that showed, as Edward Kingsley's did, the man's partiality to drink. But where Edward had grown soft and prone to mental lapses, this man looked tough and alert and very, very dangerous.

"Well, well, well," he said in a deep, Southern drawl. "Detective McClain, isn't it? Or should I say, former Detective McClain? I hear you've hit on some hard times, Jake."

"I've seen better," Jake agreed.

"And you must be Mrs. Kingsley," the man said to Hope. "I've seen your picture in the paper several times in the past. Eleanor Beaucamp's column, I believe. I'm Simon Pratt," he said with a slight bow. "And this is my associate, Jonas Thorpe." He nodded toward the man who had brought them in.

In the brighter light of the library, Thorpe looked older than Hope had originally guessed—probably somewhere in his early fifties. His superb physical condition had made him seem younger in the darkness, but now she could see the deep lines around his eyes and mouth, the broad, flat, boxer's nose, and the lack of emotion in his eyes. She shuddered as his cold gaze fell upon her.

"I don't believe you two have met," Pratt said to Jake. "Jonas came to me a few months ago by way of Houston. He's quickly making himself indispensable in my organization. Isn't that right, Jonas?"

Jonas's gaze never left Hope's. "I do what I can."

"And you do it very well," Pratt added. "Very efficiently." He lifted the top from a burled walnut humidor and removed a long, fat cigar. Holding it to his nose, he closed his eyes and inhaled. "Take Mrs. Kingsley to the solarium, Jonas. Entertain her for a while. I'd like a word with my old friend here."

Jonas's eyes darkened on Hope. "My pleasure."

Jake made a move in protest, but the gun in Jonas's hand flashed again. "Don't try it," Pratt advised. "Jonas, here, would like nothing better than to put a bullet between your eyes. He has a very itchy trigger-finger, I'm told."

"It's all right," Hope said softly to Jake. The thought of Jake getting shot made her feel sick. She stepped away from him and followed Jonas out of the room.

When the door closed behind them, Jake turned back to Pratt. From the window behind Pratt's desk, he could see one of the guards making his rounds with a Doberman. The dog looked huge in the darkness.

"You don't need to worry about Mrs. Kingsley." Pratt eyed him with dark, knowing eyes. "Jonas won't make a move without my say-so. He's very reliable."

"You'd better pray he is," Jake said tightly. "If he lays one finger on her, you're both dead men."

Pratt smiled. "And they say chivalry is dead."

Jake looked at him in disgust. "What the hell is this show of muscle all about, anyway? Why'd you have us brought here?"

"You were trespassing on my property," Pratt replied. "Consider yourself lucky. Jonas usually shoots first and asks questions later."

"That itchy trigger-finger again," Jake said.

Pratt chuckled. "Precisely." He clipped off the end of his cigar, then took his time lighting up. The aromatic smell of exotic tobacco filled the room. *Cuban,* Jake noted. Pratt probably had a direct line to Castro.

"It's curious you felt the need to purchase the land where Andrew Kingsley cracked up his car," Jake commented.

"We Southerners are sentimental that way."

Jake's eyes narrowed on Pratt. "If I didn't know better, I might think you were trying to conceal something."

"After five months?" Pratt's tone sounded incredulous, his drawl even more exaggerated. "The cops have been all over that place. If there was anything to find, I'm sure they would have found it by now. Or don't you have faith in your fellow lawmen?"

"Not the ones on your payroll," Jake said.

Pratt laughed again, exhaling a thick cloud of smoke. "I see you're still trying to connect me to Andrew Kingsley's untimely demise. You've been watching too many bad movies, Jake. You'd better find yourself another job before that imagination of yours does something to your sanity."

"Oh, I don't know," Jake returned. "I like having time on my hands. Gives me plenty of opportunity to find out all kinds of interesting things. For instance, I learned not too long ago that you own controlling interest in several of the new casinos down in Mississippi—one of the few legit businesses you're involved in. Word has it Kingsley was in to you for nearly half a mil. That's a lot of money, even for a Kingsley."

"And you think, what?" Pratt questioned. "That I had him 'iced' because he reneged on his loan? You *have* been watching too many movies. I've always thought that practice made damned poor business sense, killing a man who owes you money. How do you ever recoup?''

"I also learned," Jake said, "that in the last few months before he died, Andrew made a lot of runs south of the border in the Kingsley jet, not to mention a trip or two abroad. To Ireland, to be exact, and to the Middle East. Trouble spots seemed to attract him."

"Maybe the man liked to live dangerously," Pratt replied with a shrug. "Like you, Jake." His tone was pleasant enough, but his eyes were deadly serious.

"You think you keep a low profile, living out here in no man's land, but the drug smuggling, the gun-running, the money laundering, and all the other nasty little activities you've got your filthy hands into are no secret. My theory is this. Kingsley was in to you for a lot of money. When he couldn't come up with the dough, you made him a deal, one he couldn't refuse. He became your own personal courier. The Kingsleys are renowned all over the world. Their jet would be the last place the feds and nervous little customs agents would search for contraband."

"Interesting theory." Pratt studied the glowing tip of his cigar. "Only one thing wrong with it. Why would I get rid of such a profitable arrangement? Why would I kill Andrew Kingsley?"

"Maybe because he balked," Jake said. "Or maybe you decided he knew too much. He'd outlived his usefulness."

Through the smoke, Pratt's gaze on Jake deepened. "Do you remember what I told you two years ago when you came to arrest me for murder? Play with fire and you're going to get burned. Do you remember that, Jake?''

''I remember.''

''And here you arc. A washed-up ex-cop living with his aging father. How does it feel to have lost everything? Your job, home, money. Respect.''

Jake met Pratt's gaze through the smoke. ''Are you saying you got me fired?''

Pratt smiled. ''Iris Kingsley isn't the only one with pull in this town. Though she is quite formidable, I'll admit. If I were you, I wouldn't want to cross her again. No telling what she might do if she knew you were still messing around in her dead grandson's business. Not to mention with her dead grandson's wife.''

''Is that a threat?''

''You know me better than that. I don't make threats, I make promises.'' Pratt touched a button beneath his desk and the door to the library swung open. A moment later, Hope and Jonas Thorpe walked back through. ''We're all finished in here,'' Pratt said. ''Show Jake and Mrs. Kingsley out, will you, Jonas?''

Thorpe led them down the hallway, into the foyer. ''Do I get my gun back?'' Jake asked.

The guard handed Thorpe the weapon. With a smooth, practiced motion, he removed the clip, then gave the gun to Jake.

''Thanks a lot,'' Jake said, shoving the gun under his belt.

Thorpe opened the front door and stepped outside with them. ''Your truck is just down the road a ways,'' he said. ''Mr. Pratt thought you might enjoy a nice walk this evening. Careful of the dogs, though.'' Then he turned and disappeared back inside the house.

Hope turned to Jake. "What was that all about?"

"I'm not sure. But I think we may be getting a little too close for Pratt's comfort."

"Close to what?"

"I haven't figured that out yet," he admitted. "Come on. Let's get going."

The road wound through the woods, and the thick canopy of leaves overhead blocked the moonlight. The darkness was almost complete. In the distance, one of the dogs bayed at the moon, and Jake sensed rather than saw Hope shiver beside him. His own nerves were on edge, as well. The blinking red lights in the trees followed their progress down the road, but those weren't the "eyes" Jake was most concerned about. Something slunk in the woods nearby.

Hoped stopped. "Listen."

"What is it?"

"The barking," she said. "It's louder."

She was right. The distant barking suddenly wasn't so distant. It was behind them and in the woods, and gaining all the time. Jake's heart tripped inside him. The dogs were loose.

He grabbed Hope's hand. "Run," he said, taking off at a sprint and pulling Hope with him.

The barking grew steadily louder. Jake could hear the sound of the dogs' paws pounding against the road behind them and tearing through the underbrush. They seemed to be coming from every direction.

Around a bend in the road, he spotted the Blazer. Beside him, Hope gave a little sob of relief. But the relief was short-lived. From the woods, one of the dogs lunged toward the road. Another sprang from the darkness behind them.

Jake drew his gun, knowing that without ammunition, it was next to useless. "Make a run for it," he told Hope. "I'll be right behind you."

Hope dashed toward the truck. The dog nearest to Jake growled in menace, ready to attack. Jake threw his gun at the beast and had the satisfaction of hearing a solid *thunk* as metal connected with flesh. The dog howled in pain and rage, only momentarily distracted from his prey. But it bought Jake a few precious seconds. He turned and raced for the truck. Hope grabbed his arm and pulled him inside. As Jake slammed the door, one of the dogs jumped from the darkness and landed on the hood of the Blazer, his long, sharp teeth threatening even through the windshield. Another dog attacked Hope's window, and yet another propelled his body toward Jake's door.

"Hurry," Hope said. "Get us out of here."

The keys weren't in the ignition. "Damn!" Jake exclaimed. Pratt had lured them to the truck and then trapped them here. No telling how long they would have to stay before he called off the dogs.

Jake bent and felt beneath the floor mat, surprised when his hand closed over the keys.

"Oh, God, hurry," Hope begged. The huge Doberman was snapping at her through the glass. Jake could hear a cracking sound every time the dog lunged.

It took him three tries to get the key in the ignition, an eternity as more dogs came tearing out of the darkness. Jake started the engine and floored the accelerator. The Blazer shot forward and the Doberman on the hood went sliding off with a yelp. The dogs at the side windows fell away, and Hope put her hand to her heart. "I've never been so frightened," she gasped.

"Yeah, it got pretty hairy back there," he said, sending her a sidelong glance

To his surprise, she laughed breathlessly. "I didn't think we had a dog's chance."

They were both laughing in nervous relief when the Blazer rounded the last curve in the drive and they were suddenly at the gate. A closed and locked gate.

Hope glanced behind them. "They're coming," she said. "I think I can see them." She turned back around. "What do we do now?"

"Good question," Jake said.

"Can you ram it?"

"Not a good idea," he said. "That metal's solid. We may have to scale it instead."

Hope stared at him in horror. "You mean get out of the truck?"

"It may be our only chance." But just then, like magic, the gates slid open before them. "Voilá," Jake said. "I guess Pratt has a sense of humor after all."

JAKE DROPPED HOPE OFF at her car at the Club Mystique, then followed her home. He wasn't about to let her out of his sight until she was safely behind locked doors, he told her. And Hope had to admit that after the harrowing experience the two of them had just shared, it was comforting to have Jake so nearby.

At the gate to the Kingsley property, he waited until she was safely inside and the gates had closed behind her before he drove around to the rear entrance where the servants and delivery people entered the estate. Hope pulled her own car around the circular drive in front of the mansion and parked, knowing someone would later move the vehicle to the garages, where it would be washed and refueled for the next time she wanted to take a drive.

Hope had never been comfortable having servants at her beck and call, and she hated it even more now as she watched Jake's headlights move toward the rear of the property. Her mother was right, Hope thought, as she let herself inside the house. The sooner she moved out of the mansion, the better.

The lights on the ground floor had been lowered, with only wall sconces and an occasional lamp to chase away the gloom. Hope moved into the library, intent on pouring herself a brandy to take upstairs with her. Her nerves still weren't what they should be, and she needed something that would brace her for the long night ahead, when shock was bound to set in.

Splashing a generous amount of liquor into a snifter, Hope lifted the glass to her lips. Only then did she see the silhouette of a man standing by the windows, in a shadow that was lcft untouched by the lamp she'd turned on.

She gasped and the snifter fell from her hand. The silhouette separated from the other shadows and moved toward her, tall and lean and somehow menacing in the meager light.

Or perhaps, Hope thought, her mind was still on the dogs. After all, Jeremy had never frightened her before. He was a bore, yes, and odd, to say the least, but harmless.

His gaze dropped to the spilled brandy at her feet. "Hope," he said. "What's wrong?"

"Nothing. You startled me, that's all." He was dressed for bed in a dark blue robe over light gray pajamas. It struck Hope that she had never seen Jeremy in anything but a suit.

"You look different," he said, echoing her thoughts. "Your hair is all messed up."

She forced a soft laugh, running her fingers through the tangles. "Oh, that. I was driving with the top down."

"It's cool out. Weren't you wearing a jacket?"

"It's not that cool," she said. "Besides, I didn't go far."

"You've been gone for hours."

Hope frowned. "Are you keeping tabs on me, Jeremy?"

He looked a bit flustered. "No, it's not that. I mean, I just happened to notice…" His voice trailed away and his gaze dropped. He seemed fixated on her jeans.

Hope's frown deepened. She didn't think she cared much for this new attention from Jeremy. Or had it been there all along, even when Andrew was alive, and she just hadn't noticed?

She bent to retrieve the glass. "I'd better get something to clean up this mess," she said, wanting to escape.

"Leave it," Jeremy said carelessly. "Someone will take care of it in the morning."

"The stain will have set by then. I'll see what I can find in the kitchen. No sense you waiting up, though," she added as she turned to leave.

"Hope?"

She paused and glanced back at him.

"I thought I saw other headlights down by the gate just now. They went around back."

She lifted a brow. "So?"

"So I wondered if you'd been with Jake McClain tonight."

"Why would you wonder that?" Hope asked, in what she hoped was an innocent tone.

Jeremy's gaze deepened on her. "You used to be engaged to him."

"That was a long time ago."

"You were in love with him. I used to see you with him at his father's cottage."

Oh, no, Hope thought. Had Jeremy been spying on them back then? The notion sent a wave of heat rushing through her. The first time she and Jake had made love was at his father's cottage, in Jake's old bedroom, one afternoon while his father had been out. They'd both had apartments back then, but with roommates. Privacy had been hard to come by, so when they'd found themselves alone in the cottage that afternoon, temptation had prevailed.

They'd left the bedroom window open, and the air had been filled with the scent of flowers from the gardens. Hope had thought it all so very romantic, but now she remembered something else. A tree with wide limbs grew near Jake's window, and as she and Jake had lain naked in his bed, Hope had thought for one split second that she'd seen something moving in those branches. A flash of pale skin...

Jeremy had been a grown man even then. The notion of his deliberately watching her and Jake made Hope feel nauseous. She'd always felt a little sorry for Jeremy, but now she suspected there was more to him than met the eye. She wondered if his quiet demeanor was nothing more than a carefully constructed facade to mask what her mother would call a sly and crafty nature.

"I don't care to discuss my relationship with Jake," she said coolly.

"No, of course." But he looked a little hurt by her rebuff. Or was that anger glinting in his gray eyes?

"Well, good night," Hope forced herself to say politely. "I guess I'll see you in the morning."

"Yes," Jeremy replied, with a curious little smile. "I'm sure you will."

Chapter Seven

Late Saturday afternoon, Hope was in her suite at the mansion, getting ready for Brant Colter's wedding, when Iris knocked on the door. She looked surprised, and none too pleased, to see Hope dressed to go out.

"I was hoping we could have tea together." Iris was groomed as impeccably as ever, but she no longer wore black. Her mourning attire had been dispensed with shortly after Michael Eldridge had entered their lives. Today she was dressed in a jade pants-and-tunic outfit, complemented by a breathtaking diamond-and-emerald brooch. "Michael's coming by later."

Hope was glad she had a legitimate excuse for being absent from the house during his visit. "I'm sorry, but I've made plans with my mother for the evening." No use telling Iris what those plans were. Mentioning Brant Colter's name was bound to stir up painful memories for her, since it had been Brant's uncle who had confessed to kidnapping Adam.

"I understand." Iris sat down on the edge of Hope's bed and watched her put the finishing touches to her makeup. "You look lovely, my dear. I've always thought that color was very becoming to you."

"Thank you," Hope said, inspecting the lavender

silk dress in the mirror. Was it too short? She was thirty-two, after all. Hardly matronly, but not an ingenue any longer. Opening the lid of her jewelry box, she withdrew a strand of pearls that Andrew had given her for one of their anniversaries, the year he'd gotten himself the Porsche.

Hope held the necklace to her dress. "Yes," Iris said approvingly. "Pearls are always appropriate."

Hope fastened them around her neck, then picked up her bag. "Well," she said, "I guess I'm off, then."

"I'll give Michael your regards," Iris said.

Please don't, Hope thought, but she merely smiled at Iris before she turned to exit the room.

Hope's car had been brought around a little while earlier, and as she descended the steps to the walkway, she saw the red Viper rounding the last curve in the drive. Michael was early.

Hope hurried across the cobblestone drive to the Jaguar, intent on making a getaway before he could reach the house. But Michael must have spotted her and accelerated, because before she could climb inside her car, he screeched to a halt in front of the house and hopped out.

"Hello," he called. "Where are you off to all dressed up?"

Hope hesitated. Politeness dictated that she wait and make small talk with him, no matter how uneasy he made her. She glanced up at the house. A curtain moved in Iris's sitting-room window. She was up there watching them, Hope realized.

"I'm meeting my mother," she said noncommittally.

He walked toward her. "I love that dress," he said, propping one arm on the Jaguar's top.

"Thank you." Hope glanced at her watch. "I hate to dash off like this, but I am running late."

"Oh, well, in that case." He straightened, tapping the Jaguar affectionately. "We wouldn't want to keep Joanna waiting, now would we?"

He strolled off with his hands in his pockets, whistling some inane tune as Hope stared after him, her heart pounding and her mouth going dry. She got into the car, but her hands were shaking so badly she couldn't turn the ignition. How had he known her mother's name? There was no way, unless…

Hope closed her eyes. *It can't be,* she told herself. What she was thinking was incredible. Someone—Iris, maybe—must have mentioned her mother's name to Michael. That was the only possible explanation.

But he'd used it so casually, so naturally, as if he'd spoken her mother's name dozens of times before.

"Andrew is dead," Hope whispered aloud. He had to be. Nothing else made sense. Why would he fake his own death, then deliberately pretend to be someone else? It would take a madman to try and pull off such a bizarre stunt.

Or a desperate one…

She stopped suddenly, as Jake's words came rushing back to her. *"Andrew owed Pratt a lot of money. One way or another, Pratt always collects."*

Could Andrew have fabricated his own death in order to escape Pratt's wrath? Hope had met the man, had seen firsthand what he was capable of. She could well imagine Andrew's desperation.

But to perpetrate such an elaborate hoax would take

a great deal of planning. Not to mention conspirators. Someone would have had to help him. Someone with a great deal of money and power, Hope thought suddenly, her gaze returning to Iris's sitting-room window.

"Oh, Hope. Don't you see? It's as if Andrew's come back to us," Iris had told her the first day Michael had visited the mansion. And now Iris was no longer wearing black. No longer in mourning. She had even begun to hint that Hope and Michael...

Hope put trembling hands to her face. Did Iris know something no one else did? Was that why she had taken to Michael so quickly? Was that why she didn't want him investigated?

No, Hope thought. She couldn't believe that. She'd seen how grief-stricken Iris had been when she'd learned of Andrew's death. There was no way she could have been pretending. Unless, of course, she hadn't yet known...

Stop it! Hope commanded herself firmly. *Andrew is dead. Dead and buried, and that's that.*

But as she reached for the ignition, she caught a glimpse of her reflection in the rearview mirror. Her image seemed to be mocking her, reminding her that for over thirty years, *Adam* Kingsley was thought to have been dead and buried, too.

And they'd been wrong about him.

BY THE TIME HOPE and her mother arrived at the church, Hope had managed to convince herself once again that her imagination was simply running away with her. There was something odd about Michael Eldridge, no question. He seemed to be deliberately trying to make her think he was Andrew. His mannerisms. The cologne. And now mentioning her mother's name. But whatever sick game he was playing, Hope wanted no part of it. And by allowing herself to think for even one minute that Andrew could still be alive was playing right into the man's possibly psychotic hands.

"Isn't it a perfect evening for a wedding?" Joanna asked as she linked her arm through Hope's. "You look so pretty tonight, Hope. You could be a bride yourself."

"Don't start," Hope warned as they neared the church. But her mother was right. The day had been glorious, mild and sunny, and now twilight had fallen like the softest of blankets over the churchyard. The early stars burned in the eastern sky, bright and steadfast, and just barely visible over the horizon, the moon was rising like some ancient silver disk that had been polished a bit too thin around the edges.

The air smelled deliciously of cherry blossoms, roses and hyacinths. Wisteria plunged purple over the brick wall surrounding the church, and high in the gnarled branches of a locust tree, doves came home to roost, cooing as sweetly as an old love song.

It was a perfect evening for a wedding. A perfect night for romance.

Glancing up, Hope saw Jake at the entrance to the church. He wore dark gray pleated trousers with a sport coat and a white shirt, but no tie. He stood talking to some of the men gathered just outside the door, but as Hope and her mother approached, his gaze locked onto hers and Hope's breath left her in a painful rush.

She thought suddenly of the way he had kissed her two nights before. Gently, almost wistfully. And yet there had been a hint even then of something more. Something deeper. Something…hotter.

Passion had never been in short supply between them, she remembered. They'd once had it all.

"There's Jake," her mother whispered. "Why don't you go say hello?"

Joanna's voice seemed to break the spell. Hope tore her gaze from Jake's and glared down at her mother. "Mother, don't."

Joanna's brows rose in innocence. "What? All I did was suggest you go say hello to an old friend. What's so wrong with that?"

"You know exactly what's wrong with it," Hope replied. "You're doing it again. Trying to get Jake and me together, and I want you to stop."

Joanna let out a long, exasperated breath. "Why do you keep doing this to yourself, Hope? Why do you keep torturing yourself out of some misplaced loyalty to Andrew? You made a mistake ten years ago, but you've been bound and determined all this time not to admit it. I could admire that to a point. God knows, I'm no fan of divorce. A part of me has always been very proud of the way you fought to make your marriage work. But enough is enough, already. Andrew is dead, and there's no point in pretending anymore. Now go on over there and say hello to Jake, before it's too late."

"Too late for what?"

Joanna's mouth tightened into a thin, disapproving line. "See for yourself," she said, nodding toward the entrance of the church.

Hope followed her gaze. Jake was still among the group of men gathered at the door, but a newcomer had joined them. Sissy McDonnell, a recent divorcée, had established herself at Jake's side and latched on to his arm as if she never intended to relinquish it. Hope remembered Sissy from college. She'd been something of a femme fatale even back then, and she'd always had a crush on Jake.

Seeing them together, Hope experienced an unpleasant sensation in the pit of her stomach. A sour taste in the back of her mouth.

"See what I mean?" Joanna nudged Hope with her purse. "A man like that won't wait forever."

AS JAKE TOOK HIS SEAT inside the church, he noticed that Hope sat two pews up and across the aisle from him, which allowed him a view of her profile every time she turned to speak to her mother. Her hair was pulled back from her face and fastened in the back with a pearl clasp, giving her an air of sophistication and elegance. But the lavender dress she wore was just plain sexy. Jake had always loved Hope in lavender.

She'd worn that color the first time they met, at the police department's yearly picnic in Overton Park. He'd been a rookie, fresh out of the academy, with a confidence that bordered on arrogance. "More brawn than brains" had been Hope's first impression of him, she'd later told him.

Dan Sterling, Hope's father and Jake's immediate supervisor, had called him over and introduced him to his wife and daughter. Joanna had immediately taken him under her wing, clucking and fawning over him like a mother hen, introducing him around and making sure he got enough to eat.

Hope, on the other hand, had remained intriguingly aloof all day, reading a book or sitting alone, quietly watching all the rookies make fools of themselves, drinking too much, talking too loud, and trying to out muscle the more seasoned officers in a baseball game.

She'd been wearing white shorts with a lavender top that did incredible things to her eyes, and as Jake rounded the bases after hitting his third homer, he saw her watching him from the bleachers. He nearly missed home plate. When he came back into the dug-out, he pointed her out to Brant Colter, another rookie.

"Hope Sterling? Forget it," Brant had said. "You're not her type."

"Oh, yes, I am," Jake assured him. "I'm exactly her type. I'm going to marry that girl someday."

Well, "someday" had never arrived, Jake thought now, staring at Hope's profile. "Someday" had re-mained as elusive as a dream that he couldn't recall the next morning.

The wedding march sounded, and everyone stood, turning expectantly to catch the first glimpse of the bride. Valerie entered the chapel slowly, on the arm of her father, a man who had spent over thirty years in prison for a crime he didn't commit. Everyone in-side the church was familiar with their story, and Jake suspected there wasn't a dry eye in the place as the two of them walked down the aisle side by side. He saw Joanna openly dab at her eyes, while beside her, Hope's face held an expression of such longing that it tore at Jake's heart.

Was her sadness for Valerie and her father? For all the time that had been lost to them?

Or was her emotion more personal than that? Was she remembering her own wedding? Jake wondered. Or the wedding that had never been?

Was she thinking, like him, of another time and another place? That elusive "someday"...

THE RECEPTION WAS HELD in a community center within walking distance of the church. Hope only intended to stay for a few minutes, just long enough to congratulate Brant and give her best wishes to Valerie. The two of them seemed so happy, so much in love that it was almost painful to witness.

But then before she could make her exit, it was time for the bride and groom's first dance together. Then everyone started dancing, and before Hope knew it, she was swept onto the floor by first one old acquaintance, then another, and she spent the remainder of the evening reminiscing and feeling more relaxed than she had in a long time.

Maybe she still did belong here, she thought wistfully. After all these years, maybe she could still come home.

"Mind if I cut in?" said a deep voice over her partner's shoulder—a voice Hope knew as well as she knew her own. A shiver of pleasure raced through her as she looked up to meet Jake's gaze.

George Bailey, another cop who had been under her father's command, frowned, his arms tightening around Hope. "Get lost, McClain."

"Your wife's looking for you," Jake said.

George shrugged. "Which one?"

"The current one."

George stopped abruptly. "Jeez, Karen's here?"

Jake motioned toward the doorway. "Over there somewhere."

"If you're lying to me, McClain..." George's gaze

scanned the room nervously before he took off in the direction Jake had sent him.

For a moment, Jake and Hope stood facing each other. Then he smiled. "Dance?"

"You used to hate to dance," she said.

He shrugged. "Times change. People change."

Hope walked into his arms and felt them close around her. Her eyes drifted shut for a moment, absorbing the sensations spiraling through her. Excitement. Attraction. And yes, even a little fear.

She shivered, and Jake pulled her even closer. Hope thought she caught a glimpse of her mother's beaming face in the crowd, but she quickly dismissed it. She didn't want anything, even her mother's good intentions, intruding on this moment. Because if she tried hard enough, Hope could almost pretend the last ten years had never happened. She could almost believe she and Jake were still together, and that she had worn this lavender dress just for him.

And maybe she had.

"Is George's wife really here?" she asked.

Jake grinned. "One of them is bound to be."

"How many times has he been married? I've lost count."

"We all have. You have to give him points for trying, though."

"You never did."

"What?"

"You never tried marriage," Hope said. "Why not?"

He hesitated, then said, "I almost did. Twice."

Hope gazed up at him. "What happened? The second time, I mean."

He shrugged. "I guess it was pretty much the same thing that happened the first time. She decided she couldn't be a cop's wife after I got shot that time. I don't know if you remember it or not."

Hope remembered, all right. She and Andrew had been out of the country, vacationing on the Côte d'Azur. She didn't find out about the shooting until a month later when they returned home. Even though Jake was okay by then, Hope had been devastated by the news. Rather than telling herself that it only proved she'd been right to call off their engagement, all Hope could think was that while she'd been lying on a beach on the Riviera, Jake had been lying in the hospital, fighting for his life. He could have died, and her not there.

Hope sighed without meaning to.

"It's warm in here," Jake said. "Let's get some air."

They walked outside to the little courtyard in back of the community center. The moon was up now, but veiled by a thin filigree of clouds. A light breeze drifted through the trees, stirring the scent of the wisteria.

"Nice night," Jake murmured.

"Very," Hope agreed. She shivered a bit in the breeze. "Valerie and Brant seem so happy, don't they?"

"Yeah. Especially considering what they've been through."

"I remember when the story broke last summer,"

Hope said. "We couldn't believe Cletus Brown, Valerie's father, had been proved innocent after all those years. In all the excitement over the discovery that Adam might still be alive, I just kept thinking about Brant—what all of that must have done to his family. To him. He had to shoot his own cousin in order to save Valerie's life. Sometimes I wonder what it would be like to have someone love you that much—"

Jake stared down at her in the moonlight. "You had that once," he said with a bitter edge in his voice. "I would have done anything for you back then."

"Except give up being a cop," Hope said softly.

He hesitated. "Yeah. Except that." Maybe it was her imagination, but Hope thought the bitterness in his voice had turned to regret.

She glanced up at him. "Is there a chance you could ever go back? To being a cop, I mean."

Jake shook his head. "The board's decision was final, and besides, I don't feel the same about the department anymore. I could never go back."

Hope smiled wistfully in the moonlight. "I know what you mean. Earlier, when I was inside with George and David and Sarah and all the others I knew from the old neighborhood, I got to thinking that maybe things hadn't changed that much. That maybe I did still belong here, but..." She trailed off with a shrug. "Ten years is a long time. I guess it's true what they say. You can never really go home."

"Maybe not," Jake said. "Maybe that wouldn't be the healthiest thing to do anyway. Living in the past rarely is. Maybe what you and I should do is concentrate on the present. On what we feel now."

Hope's heart accelerated. Her stomach fluttered with awareness. "I don't—"

"Be honest, Hope. There is something between us."

"I wasn't going to deny it," she said softly. "I was going to say, I don't know how I feel."

"That's okay." Jake smiled down at her in the soft, filtered light. "No one's rushing you. We've got all the time in the world to figure it out."

Did they? Suddenly Hope wanted more than anything to believe it was so. To forget that there was a man out there who looked exactly like her husband, a man named Michael Eldridge who might be waiting for the opportunity to destroy the fragile bond she and Jake were just now attempting to rebuild.

He bent to kiss her and Hope closed her eyes, a storm of emotions washing over her. Not sadness this time. Not regret or remorse or thoughts of what might have been. When Jake kissed her this time, it was like a first kiss. Like the promise of a new beginning.

Hope parted her lips and let her tongue gently mate with Jake's. Tightening his arms around her, he pulled her close, until their bodies melted together and the kiss deepened. The sensations rushing through Hope intensified. The night suddenly came alive with their passion.

Jake pulled back long enough to whisper her name in the darkness, a dusky entreaty that sent shivers of desire up and down Hope's back. Then his mouth claimed hers again, hungrier this time, more demanding. His hands moved over her, and everywhere he touched set Hope on fire.

My God, she thought in a daze. It had never been like this before, had it? How could she have given this up?

A touch of longing swept through her, shadowing the desire. How had she done without this man's kiss, this man's touch for ten long years? How had she managed to convince herself, even for a moment, that she and Jake were not meant to be?

As if sensing her mood, Jake broke the kiss and pulled away to stare down at her in the moonlight. He pushed back her hair from her face with a hand that was exquisitely gentle, but his eyes were still dark and intense, still burning with passion.

"I'm not sure what I'm supposed to say here," he murmured huskily.

Hope managed a weak smile. "Me, neither."

"I didn't plan for that to happen, you know." His tone turned ironic. "Then again, I feel as if I've been waiting for it most of my life. Ten years, at least."

"Jake—"

"I'm not trying to rush you, Hope. I know it hasn't been that long since Andrew died."

At the mention of her husband, a shadow seemed to creep over the courtyard. Hope shivered in Jake's arms. "No, it hasn't," she said, gently pulling away from him.

Jake let her go, watching her with hooded eyes. "You still have feelings for him, don't you? Even though you wanted to divorce him."

"I'm not sure how I feel about Andrew anymore," Hope answered truthfully. She stepped away from Jake and the wind suddenly grew colder, the courtyard darker, the shadows more menacing at the mention of her husband's name.

A premonition of dread slipped over Hope. It wasn't that she saw someone lurking in the shadows. It wasn't that she heard stealthy footfalls in the darkness. But just the same, she had the strongest sensation that someone was out there watching her. He had seen her with Jake. He'd seen them kiss. And he hadn't liked it. Not one bit.

I'll see you both dead first, the wind seemed to whisper.

A fist of fear closed around Hope's heart. What if Andrew *was* still alive? What if he'd changed his name, his identity, so that he could come back here and renew his relationship with Hope, his rivalry with an old foe? How far would he be willing to go to keep Jake from winning this time?

"It's late," she whispered. "I have to go."

Jake started to protest, but then he must have seen something in her eyes, the look on her face, for a shutter closed over his own expression. "You're right," he said. "It is late."

Maybe too late, his tone seemed to imply.

JAKE STOOD OUTSIDE his father's cottage, on the edge of the Kingsley grounds, and stared up at the house. How many times had he done this same thing as a child? Stared at the Kingsley mansion from a distance, trying to imagine all the riches within.

There was only one treasure inside that house he coveted now, but in many ways, Hope was still just as unattainable to him as she had been for the past ten years. Something was still coming between them—Andrew's memory, Jake suspected—and there wasn't a damn thing he could do about it. How could you compete with a ghost?

His gaze went to the west wing of the house, where Hope's suite was located. A light shone from one of the windows, and Jake watched, hoping to catch a glimpse of her inside.

And then suddenly she was there, a dark silhouette in the window, staring out at the garden. At him, he wanted to imagine.

"She's very beautiful," a voice said from the darkness.

Jake whirled, tense and alert. How the hell had he let someone slip up on him like that?

You're losing it, McClain. In more ways than one. For a moment there, he'd thought the voice sounded like Andrew's, and the hair on the back of Jake's neck stood on end.

"Who's there?" he said.

The grounds around his father's cottage lay in deep shadow. Jake peered into the gloom from where the disembodied voice had spoken. All was silent, and for a split second, he thought he must have imagined the voice. Then slowly, the shadows stirred and a man stepped into the moonlight.

Jake's mouth went completely dry as he stared at the apparition before him. Then, almost instantly, relief washed over him. Not Andrew after all, but the would-be heir prowling the Kingsley grounds.

"You must be Eldridge," Jake said.

The man continued to move toward him, but

stopped a few feet away from Jake, as if he didn't want to be examined too closely in the moonlight. He smiled Andrew's smile, his gaze going to the lighted window in the mansion. "You were watching her."

Jake shrugged. "What if I was?"

Michael's eyes never left Hope's window. Without meaning to, Jake followed his gaze. Hope remained at the window, and he wondered if she could see the two of them out here in the darkness. Watching her.

"A woman like her would be hard to forget." Jake turned and found Eldridge's gaze on him now. There was something in his eyes that sent a cold chill straight through Jake's heart. "I imagine a man would be willing to do just about anything to hold on to someone like her."

Chapter Eight

After church the next morning, Hope drove across town toward the airport to meet Jake at his office. He'd called earlier, telling her in a low voice that he had some information about "the situation." But he hadn't wanted to tell her over the phone, nor had he wanted to meet on the grounds, and Hope had agreed. She didn't want anyone overhearing the conversation and reporting back to Iris before they had all the facts.

The lobby and most of the offices were deserted as Hope entered the building and took the elevator up to the third floor. Jake's door stood ajar when she arrived, and she knocked gently before pushing it open and peering inside.

As usual, Jake sat at his computer. He stood when he saw her and motioned her inside. When they were both seated—she on one of the leather chairs and he on the edge of his desk—he told her what he'd learned.

"Michael Eldridge has a record."

Hope stared at him in surprise. "You mean he's been in prison?"

"Juvenile detention. He was arrested for breaking and entering at the age of fifteen. Actually, the records were sealed when he turned eighteen, but I have a friend in the Houston Police Department who used to work with me here in town. She stuck her neck out for me and got into the files."

Hope frowned. "You just found this out today? On Sunday morning?"

"Actually, Sunday morning is the best time to use the computers at a police department," Jake explained. "Not as many prying eyes. But I knew about this last night."

"Why didn't you tell me?" Hope demanded. She thought about the way she'd felt in the courtyard, as if someone was watching her from the darkness. And now to find out that Michael Eldridge had a record...

"I started to," Jake said. "But somehow a wedding didn't seem the appropriate place. And then other things...distracted me."

Their kiss, Hope remembered, feeling her face heat in spite of herself. For a while last night, she had felt as close to Jake as she ever had. Maybe even closer. Then her doubts about Andrew had intruded, and the moment had ended—torn asunder by her fear.

She glanced at Jake now, his expression solemn, his eyes cool, and she wondered if she should try to explain. *The reason I ran out on you last night was because I thought my dead husband was watching us from the shadows. I thought he might try to kill you. You know how competitive he always was.*

Hope cringed inwardly. She would sound insane. And maybe she was.

She cleared her throat. "Having a record may make him look suspicious, but it still doesn't tell us whether or not he's an impostor."

"No, but it's a start," Jake said. "And there's one

other thing. His lawyer was a man named Charles McGee. He was a partner at Northrup, Simmons and Fitzgerald before he died last year in a car crash. He was recruited by the firm shortly after he defended Michael, and he made partner a few years later.''

"So what does that mean?" Hope asked.

Jake shrugged. "Maybe nothing. But I don't much believe in coincidences. Supposing this Charles McGee saw Andrew Kingsley one day after McGee started working at the firm. Wouldn't be surprising. The firm has managed all the Kingsley holdings for years now. Supposing he just happened to mention to someone—Victor Northrup, say, or even Jeremy Willows, who clerked at the firm that year—that he had a client in Houston who bore an amazing resemblance to Andrew Kingsley.''

"And?"

"It's an interesting little tidbit," Jake continued, "Filed away in someone's memory and all but forgotten until years later when *bam!* It's discovered that *Adam* Kingsley may still be alive.''

"So you're saying that either Victor or Jeremy then remembered Charles McGee's client down in Houston and, what? Thought he might be the real Adam Kingsley?"

"Just the opposite," Jake said. "They thought he might be able to *pretend* to be Adam Kingsley until he could get his hands on the Kingsley fortune."

"But Victor Northrup is wealthy in his own right," Hope said. "He's a millionaire. And as for Jeremy—"

"He never had a prayer of being Iris's heir, did he?"

Hope shook her head. "No. She's made that very clear."

"And what would happen to Jeremy and Pamela if Edward were to die suddenly?" Jake asked. "They'd be left out in the cold unless they had a contingency plan."

Hope paused, remembering. "You may be right," she said. "I overheard Pamela and Jeremy talking one night. He asked her why she put up with Edward, and Pamela said it was only for a little while longer. I had the distinct impression that she was talking about something specific. I wondered then if they were up to something, but I never dreamed..." She trailed off, then glanced at Jake. "Do you really think they could be working with Michael?"

"I'm just saying it's a possibility," Jake said. "It's time I get down to Houston and start asking some questions. In the meantime, I think it would be better if you try to steer clear of Eldridge. Don't be alone with him. Impostor or not, there's something definitely not kosher about that guy."

WHEN HOPE ARRIVED BACK at the mansion, Iris and Michael were just sitting down to lunch on the terrace, and Iris insisted that Hope join them. Since her meeting with Jake, she was hardly in any mood for company, particularly Michael's. But it was getting harder and harder to avoid him. Hope had no choice but to sit down and admire the lovely table with its snowy linens, sparkling crystal, and fragrant bouquet of blue hyacinths.

Iris picked daintily at her shrimp-and-avocado salad, stealing not-so-surreptitious glances at Hope and Michael, until Hope became even more uncomfortable. Finally, when the chocolate-and-raspberry dessert had been served, Iris said, "We have a surprise for you, Hope."

Hope flinched, her gaze going automatically to Michael's. She couldn't imagine—didn't want to imagine—what the two of them had cooked up. What it might have to do with her.

Michael smiled, but his expression seemed distant today, his dark blue eyes cool, as if she'd done something that had displeased him. Instantly Hope flashed back to last night, to thc kiss she and Jake had shared at the reception. Had Michael seen them? Had his presence been the one she'd sensed in the courtyard?

If he really was Michael Eldridge, or an impostor, or even Adam Kingsley, there was no reason why he would care who she kissed. Why he would care about her at all.

But if he wasn't Michael Eldridge...

"I've invited Michael to move into the mansion," Iris was saying. "And he has agreed."

Hope's gaze shot to Iris, then back to Michael. He watched her intently. His eyes had a dark and edgy quality about them, as if he were contemplating something Hope was better off not knowing. He seemed different today, less like Andrew. Darker somehow, and more mysterious. More dangerous.

It occurred to Hope that he was not a man she would want to cross, and she wondered with a shiver if he had somehow found out that she'd hired Jake to investigate him. If that was why he was upset with her.

"When are you moving in?" she asked.

"Today," Iris replied for him. "The sooner the better."

"Why the rush?" Hope asked cautiously, but she could tell from the slight frown creasing Iris's brow that her comment wasn't the one Iris had hoped to hear.

"Why wait? I know what the DNA tests will tell us. Michael is my grandson. I have no doubts about that."

The smile Michael flashed Iris was the first sign of warmth Hope had seen from him since she'd arrived. He genuinely seemed to care about Iris, and Hope thought how wonderful it would be if he really was Adam. If he turned out to be exactly the kind of grandson Iris needed. Then Hope could move out of the mansion and qet on with her own life. She wouldn't have to worry about impostors and long-lost heirs and a dead husband who couldn't seem to stay in his grave.

"If you're happy," she said to Iris, "that's all that matters." She could feel Michael's gaze on her, but she didn't glance in his direction again.

Iris said, "I am happy, my dear. Ecstatically happy. There's only one thing that could possibly make me any happier." She paused and reached across the table to take Hope's hand. With her other hand, she reached for Michael's. For a moment, Hope had the wild notion that Iris might try to bring their hands together, but mercifully, she spared them that. Instead she said, "I think it would be nice if you would show Michael around the city today, Hope. Let him get to know Memphis the way we know it. I'm sure he'll come to love it as much as we do."

Hope started to protest, but Michael said quickly, "That's a wonderful idea. Hope, would you mind?"

Of course, she minded, Hope thought. She minded

a lot, but Iris was obviously waiting for her answer while Michael Eldridge's dark eyes seemed to hold a challenge. A dare. He thought Hope would be too frightened to spend the afternoon with him, but it occurred to her that it might be the perfect opportunity to trip him up. Or at the very least, learn something about him that Jake could follow up on later.

Jake's warning flashed through her mind, but Hope dismissed it. It was broad daylight, after all. What could happen? "I think it's a great idea," she said, with as much enthusiasm as she could muster. "I'd love to show you around Memphis."

As soon as Hope left his office, Jake drove back across town to his father's cottage to pack a small bag and make arrangements for his trip to Houston. There were several Southwest Airlines flights leaving Memphis International Airport that afternoon for Houston, but most of them had stops in either Little Rock or Dallas. He booked a seat on the only direct flight available—one leaving at five o'clock that afternoon, which gave him plenty of time to give his father a hand in the gardens.

Changing into a disreputable pair of jeans and a cotton shirt he left untucked and unbuttoned, Jake went in search of his father, finally locating him at the disassembled rock garden near the reflecting pool on the front lawn.

His dad knelt on the ground, attempting to arrange the heavy rocks that hadn't yet been carried away in a pattern that escaped Jake. "Here," he said. "You tell me where you want them and I'll do the lifting."

Gerald grunted as he got to his feet. "I was doing this long before you came along, Jake."

"And you'll be doing it long after I'm gone," Jake agreed, lifting one of the rocks and setting it down near the pile his father had been working on.

"Not there," he grumbled. "You've completely ruined the symmetry."

"Okay, Pop," Jake said, hanging on to his patience by a thread. "Just tell me where."

His father pulled a sheet of paper from his pocket and spread it on one of the rocks. It was a scaled architectural drawing, complete with dimensions for the new rock garden and construction guidelines for a miniature waterfall that would be fed by underground pipes.

Jake looked up from the drawing. "You designed this, Pop?"

"Who do you think?" his father said. "Miss Iris wants the rock garden rebuilt, so it's my job to find a way to do it."

"I guess I just never stopped to consider—"

"What?" his father demanded. "That your old man's job entails more than just throwing some dirt on the ground and sticking a few plants in."

"I never thought that," Jake said. "You've had me out here digging in the dirt since I was old enough to carry a spade. I guess I just never stopped to think that you were the one who designed all this." He glanced around the complex series of gardens, the color scheme and layout of each blending and complementing the next. His father was more than a gardener, Jake realized. He was an artist, and the Kingsley gardens were his painting. A giant canvas of living, blooming color.

"You really are something, Pop," Jake said quietly.

His father bent down to examine one of the rocks. "Yeah, well, if you're going to help me, help me," he said gruffly. "Don't stand out here jawing at me all day."

But it was a nice moment, and for a long time afterward, they worked in companionable silence. After an hour or so, Jake stood to stretch his back. He'd been doing all the lifting, and his muscles were starting to feel the strain. While he walked around, getting the kinks out, the front door of the mansion opened and Hope and Michael Eldridge emerged.

After what he'd told Hope about Eldridge this morning, Jake had thought she would stay as far away from him as she could, at least until they learned a few more facts about him. But here the two of them were, acting just as chummy as could be. What the hell was going on here?

Hope wore a violet dress of some flowing fabric that swirled around her tanned, slender legs as she and Michael descended the steps to the walkway. As Jake watched, he saw Eldridge put a proprietary arm around Hope's waist, and she didn't seem to object. Eldridge guided her around the Viper and helped her inside. Then he went around to the other side and climbed behind the wheel.

The two of them left without a glance in Jake's direction.

HOPE TRIED TO HIT MOST of the touristy spots with Michael. Safe, well-populated areas like Overton Square, Beale Street, Graceland, and Mud Island. Then, over drinks in the Peabody Hotel, they watched the famous Peabody ducks leave the fountain in the lobby and waddle off to the elevator, where they would be transported skyward to their penthouse suite.

Hope glanced at her watch. It was just after five, and she wondered if Jake had left for Houston yet. "Well," she said brightly, "I think we've covered just about everything."

"Not quite." Michael leaned across the table toward her, his dark blue eyes glinting with something Hope couldn't define. "I'd like to see where you grew up."

"There's not much to see," Hope said, trying to hide her surprise. Andrew had never liked going back to her old neighborhood, even to visit her mother. He'd felt uncomfortable there, like a fish out of water. Maybe this was a good sign, Hope decided. A sign that Michael Eldridge was the man he claimed to be. "The house I grew up in is nothing like the Kingsley mansion," she warned. "My father was a policeman, and my mother's a librarian."

"I know."

Hope glanced at him warily. "How do you know?"

He shrugged. "Iris and I have had many long conversations. She really loves you, you know. You're like a granddaughter to her."

"I'm very fond of her, too," Hope said. "I wouldn't want to see her get hurt. She was devastated after Andrew's death. I don't know if she could take another shock like that."

"Is that why you dislike me?" he asked. "Because you think I'm going to hurt Iris?"

His expression was earnest enough, but there was something in his eyes that bothered Hope. Had always bothered Hope. "Let's get one thing straight," she said. "I'm going to do everything in my power to make sure that you—that *no one* takes advantage of her. She's vulnerable right now, but I'm not."

"Aren't you?" His gaze grew slightly mocking. "You just lost your husband, Hope. I would think you would be extremely vulnerable at the moment."

"Then you would be wrong." She met his gaze with a long, penetrating stare of her own.

Finally, the mocking glint left his eyes, and his expression grew more serious. "You have no reason to distrust me. I've never claimed to be Adam Kingsley. Iris has made all the assumptions herself. But let me ask you this, Hope. If I am nothing but an impostor, out to get what I can from Iris, why did I subject myself to the DNA tests?"

"The results won't be back for days yet, maybe even weeks," Hope reminded him. "Already you've insinuated yourself into her affections. You've worked your way into her home. I can't help asking myself what might be next."

"Well," he said. "You're being very frank. I can appreciate that. Let me be just as open with you. I've grown to care a great deal about Iris. She's become the family I never had. It was her idea that I move into the mansion, and I was happy to comply because I've never really liked living alone. She's asked me to call her Grandmother, and I've agreed to that, too, because I asked myself, where's the harm? Especially when, for all any of us knows, I *am* her grandson. And now she has another request." His eyes deepened as he reached across the table and took Hope's hand. It required all her willpower not to flinch away. "She would like for you and me to become…close, and I have to say, I wouldn't mind that, either. You're a very attractive woman, Hope. I've been drawn to you from the first.''

His directness shattered Hope's illusion of calmness. Shocked, she drew her hand back from his, and he resisted so smoothly Hope wondered if she'd imagined the brief tightening around her fingers. "I can't believe you're saying this. We hardly know each other."

"I don't feel that way at all," he said. "I feel like I've known you for years. We share a bond...because of Andrew. He and I were identical twins, very much alike even though we weren't raised together. You must feel something for me, Hope."

The fact that they were in a public bar conducting such an intimate conversation while people talked and laughed and drank all around them made the whole scene even more surreal. Hope stared at the man across the table from her and wondered about all those long conversations he and Iris had shared. Where had he gotten the notion that Hope might want a relationship with him?

"Andrew's only been dead for five months," she began carefully.

"Yes, I know. But that only proves how fleeting life is. We shouldn't waste a moment of it."

"No one's rushing you. We've got all the time in the world to figure it out," Jake had told her. Had that only been last night?

Jake, she thought wistfully. *Where are you now when I need you?* Because in spite of Michael's earnestness, Hope still didn't trust him. She still didn't feel safe with him, and she knew instinctively that she had better handle this situation delicately. The fact that they were in a public place might not make a difference if she told Michael what she really thought of him.

"Look," he said, as if sensing her wariness. "Maybe I've gone about this all wrong. Maybe comparing myself to Andrew was the last thing I should have done. I know you two didn't have the happiest of marriages."

"And just how would you know that?" Hope asked coolly.

He shrugged. "I've picked up on some things, and I can promise you this. I may be like Andrew in a lot of ways, but I would never treat you the way he did. I wouldn't repeat his mistakes."

Hope's heart beat a painful staccato inside her. "How do you know so much about Andrew?" she whispered. "How do you know so much about me?"

His eyes grew dark and mysterious, his expression enigmatic. A smile, so much like Andrew's, tilted the corners of his mouth. "Because I'm your soul mate, Hope. Haven't you figured that out by now? You and I belong together. We always have."

Chapter Nine

Jake landed at Houston's William P. Hobby Airport shortly after six-thirty and rented a car, taking the 610 Loop to the Galleria area, a pricey district of exclusive shops, fine restaurants, and plush office buildings. The brokerage firm where Eldridge worked was located near the Southwest Freeway, and the address of his apartment, provided by the DMV, was nearby, on Westheimer, one of the city's main drags.

Traffic was heavy even for a Sunday evening, and Jake drove around for a while, getting his bearings. It was dark by the time he finally located Casa del Sol, a group of Spanish-style buildings landscaped with oleander bushes and palm trees. Colorfully described as "garden apartments," the two-story structures were not unlike the dozens of complexes that populated east Memphis.

Spotting the right building, he parked in the visitors' lot and watched the apartment for a few minutes before getting out of the car. He didn't expect trouble, but Jake was by nature and by profession a cautious man.

The buildings were stucco and brick, housing eight units each, with wrought-iron stairways at either end and a long gallery between them that provided access to the four second-story apartments.

As Jake got out of his car and started toward the building, another car pulled in and parked in the covered area reserved for the tenants. A door slammed, and in a moment, Jake heard footsteps on the metal stairs farthest from him. He took the other set of stairs, deliberately slowing his steps. As he reached the covered landing, a woman stood at the far end, outside Michael Eldridge's apartment, inserting a key into the lock.

She wore a slim yellow skirt with a matching midriff top that displayed an amazingly narrow waist, especially considering that other parts of her anatomy were just as amazingly ample. Her hair was white blond, but shiny and sleek, as if the color were natural, and when she turned to glance in his direction, Jake saw that her eyes were blue, very light and very beautiful.

"She was blond, about so high," the bartender had told him at the Club Mystique. *"And stacked. I mean, really built."*

On impulse Jake called, "Carol?"

The woman turned, then immediately realized her mistake. For a split second, she seemed to calculate her chances of getting into the apartment and slamming the door in Jake's face. But she hadn't yet unlocked the dead bolt. She whirled and took off down the stairs.

Jake tore off after her, taking the steps two at a time, then racing across the covered parking area in pursuit. She was ahead of him, but he knew he could catch her easily when she stopped to unlock her car.

As he was about to sprint the last few yards toward

her, a yellow VW streaked around the corner and into the lot, headed directly for Jake. The headlights caught him in the face, blinding him momentarily as he dived out of the way. The front fender caught his thigh as he rolled.

The car screeched to a halt and the driver jumped out. "Oh, man, are you all right? I didn't even see you." The driver was a young man, early twenties, with scruffy blond hair pulled back into a ponytail, black-rimmed glasses, baggy shorts, and an *X Files* T-shirt that proclaimed The Truth Is Out There. Techno-geek was the term that immediately came to Jake's mind.

He walked toward Jake, visibly shaken. "Oh, man," he said again. "Are you hurt?"

Jake struggled to his feet. On the other side of the VW, he heard a car door slam and the engine start up. The blonde was getting away.

The young man grabbed his arm. "You need a doctor? I can take you to the hospital."

"I'm fine," Jake said, shaking off the guy's hand. The blonde's car, a dark blue BMW with tinted windows, backed out of its slot. Jake started after her, but a searing pain shot up his leg. *"Damn,"* he swore as the BMW changed gears and shot forward, disappearing around the corner.

"Your girlfriend?" the techno-geek asked him. "What happened, the two of you have a fight?"

"Something like that," Jake muttered, hobbling back toward the apartment building.

"Listen, you sure you don't need to go to the hospital? I feel, you know, kind of responsible, here."

"I'm fine," Jake assured him. "Nothing a good stiff drink won't fix."

"Oh, well, hey. I got some Jack Daniel's in my apartment. Keep it around for when my old man visits. Never touch the stuff myself. I prefer a little reefer. It's easier on the liver."

"Thanks anyway," Jake told him.

"Well, if you're sure—" Reluctantly, the young man headed off across the parking lot toward his own apartment. Jake waited until he was inside, then retraced his steps back to Michael Eldridge's apartment.

The blonde had left the key in the dead bolt. He turned until he heard the click, then pushed open the door. Taking a penlight from his pocket, he closed the door behind him, then shone the thin beam around the room. From what he could tell, the layout was typical of such apartments. The front door opened directly into the living room with a small dining area and kitchen connected. A narrow hall led to the bathroom and one or possibly two bedrooms.

Conscious of the fact that the woman might return or send reinforcements, Jake hurriedly searched the living room, coming up with nothing. The space was neat, the furnishings conservative bordering on institutional. There was certainly nothing about the decor that even hinted at a personality partial to Vipers.

The bathroom was just as bland, yielding nothing more than a well-stocked medicine cabinet of first-aid supplies and toiletries. The first room past the bathroom was a small office with an elaborate computer system and several metal filing cabinets containing stock-market reports, investment portfolios, and computer printouts that were little more than gobbledygook to Jake.

He searched through the Rolodex on the desk, but found nothing. No name that leaped out at him. He turned on the computer and perused the directories, but again hit a dead end. It seemed that Michael Eldridge was exactly what he professed to be— a stockbroker.

The bedroom at the end of the hallway was a little more interesting, however. Here, Eldridge had allowed his imagination freer rein, decorating lavishly with animal prints, mirrors, and a video and audio system that must have cost a small fortune.

Jake searched through the dresser drawers, the nightstand, and then turned his attention to the walk-in closet, which was as ordered as the rest of the apartment. Slacks, shirts, jackets, and suits were all hung in some color-coded order, and shoe boxes had been neatly labeled and stored on shelves at the back of the closet.

Jake started with the shoe boxes. It had been his experience as a cop that shoe boxes were always the first place people used to store valuables and were, invariably, the first places crooks searched. But Eldridge's shoe boxes turned up nothing but shoes— basketball shoes, tennis shoes, boat shoes, tasseled loafers, wing tips, sandals, boots.

Jake left the closet and went back into the bedroom, shining the beam of his penlight around the room again. He walked over to the stereo and television center, scanning the expensive equipment appreciatively before checking Eldridge's musical and video selection. The music was eclectic, ranging from Steve Earle to Dead-Can-Dance, but the videos were a much narrower collection, mostly black-and-white gangster flicks from the thirties and forties.

There was a tape inside the VCR. On impulse, Jake turned on the TV, muted the volume, and pushed the

Play button on the recorder. The picture scrambled for a split second, then straightened, and to Jake's amazement, he saw Hope's face come into focus.

His heart jumped into his throat. What the hell was Hope doing on a videotape in Michael Eldridge's apartment? And it wasn't just any videotape. It was the tape of her and Andrew's wedding, shot ten years ago. The quality was strictly professional. No amateurish shaking of the camcorder, no in-and-out of focus, no shifting scenes. The lens stayed steadily on Hope as she walked slowly down the aisle, looking beautiful and radiant and so damned desirable Jake's throat tightened, just watching her.

As she neared the altar, the focus switched to Andrew, who gazed down at her with open adoration. Then he took Hope's hand, and Jake punched off the machine, not wanting to witness the vows being exchanged. He'd gone out and gotten rip-roaring drunk on Hope's wedding day ten years ago to try and block that very image. He felt like doing the same thing now, but he knew he couldn't afford the luxury. He needed all his faculties, because something was definitely not right here.

How had Eldridge gotten a videotape of Hope's wedding? What the hell was it doing here in his apartment in Houston?

But Jake knew he couldn't wait around until the answers came to him. He'd already spent too much time in the apartment, pressing his luck. He had to get out of here.

Rewinding the tape, he turned off the television and VCR, then, dousing his light at the front door, peered out the window that faced the parking lot below. The coast looked clear, so he let himself out of the apartment, leaving the key in the dead bolt where he'd found it.

"Hey!" someone yelled as he walked across the parking lot toward his car.

Jake turned to see the man in the *X Files* shirt hurrying across the pavement toward him, a bottle of Jack Daniel's in one hand and what looked like a joint in the other. He waved both at Jake.

"Smorgasbord!" The young man beamed. "Your choice of painkillers, man."

Jake reached down to unlock his car. "Thanks—"

"Benny. My name's Benny."

"Thanks, but no thanks, Benny. I'm driving."

Benny came around the side of Jake's car. "Oh, well, yeah. I can dig that. Why don't you come on back to my place? We can call up a few babes I know and have a party—"

It wasn't until Benny's gaze strayed over Jake's left shoulder then back again that Jake realized something was wrong. By then it was too late. When he started to whirl, a blow to the back of his head brought him to his knees. Pain exploded inside his head, like a thousand nails being hammered into his skull.

He tried to struggle to his feet, but only managed to fall to his side on the pavement. Standing over him, Benny nudged Jake with his foot.

"Cool," he said.

WHEN MICHAEL AND HOPE arrived home, she went straight up to her suite and stayed there for the remainder of the evening, pleading a headache so she wouldn't have to come down to dinner and face Michael again. Not that she would be able to avoid him forever. Iris had put him in the west wing, with Hope.

She shivered, thinking about her conversation with him earlier. Was it possible he really did care for her, or was this some sort of perverted machination on his part? A way to insinuate himself even more solidly into the Kingsley household?

Just after ten o'clock, Hope heard him come up to his room. She supposed that everyone else had retired for the night, and contemplated whether or not she wanted to talk to Iris now or wait until morning. If Iris had been scheming with Michael, as he'd implied, to get the two of them together, then Hope knew she had to put a stop to it right away.

She opened her door, but as she started to step out into the hallway, she heard Michael's door open as well. Hope quickly retreated back into her room, not wanting a confrontation. She closed her door, but left a tiny crack open so she could peer through.

In a moment, she saw him come down the hallway and head toward the stairs. Hope opened the door wider, listening to the sounds of his departure—footsteps on the stairs, across the foyer, and then the front door opening and closing. The faint sounds of a car engine leaping to life.

Hope stepped into the corridor, pausing. Now would be the perfect time to talk to Iris, but another thought had suddenly occurred to her. Might there be proof of Michael's true identity hidden somewhere in his room? Did she have the nerve to actually search for it?

As silent as a ghost, she slipped down the hallway to his room, hesitating as she glanced up and down the corridor. She'd never done anything remotely clandestine, and her heart pounded like a piston—not an altogether unpleasant experience. Was this sudden rush of adrenaline the kind of high Jake had experienced as a cop? Was that one of the reasons he loved his job so much?

At that moment, Hope could almost understand it. The excitement pumping through her made her almost light-headed. She had to try and calm her racing pulse.

Taking a deep breath, she reached for the knob and opened the door, stepping through quickly, then closing it softly behind her. Michael had left a light on, a small reading lamp on an antique cherry-wood desk in the corner. Hope decided the desk was as good a place as any to start her search.

But the drawers were mostly empty, and Hope wondered if Michael had even taken the time to unpack yet, which meant she would have to search through all his suitcases.

But the bureau proved more productive. He'd at least put some of his clothes away. One drawer contained neat stacks of shirts and sweaters, another socks and underwear, and the third, several pairs of running shorts. Hope searched through the sweater drawer and shorts drawer, then reluctantly came back to the socks-and-underwear drawer.

There was something about touching a stranger's intimate apparel that made her distinctly uncomfortable, but Hope knew it had to be done. Rifling as quickly as possible through the stacks of soft cotton briefs and silk boxers, she almost overlooked a framed photograph that had been shoved beneath a pile of athletic socks.

Hope pulled the picture out of the drawer and gasped, almost dropping the frame. It was a black-and-white newspaper clipping of her leaving the cemetery after Andrew's funeral. Several of the local newspapers had run the photo along with a story about Andrew's tragic death and a recapping of the Kingsley family's rise and fall in politics.

Her hands shaking, Hope stared down at her image. Beneath the wide-brimmed black hat, her face looked pale and drawn, very solemn, but there was something in her eyes, an emotion the casual observer would undoubtedly mistake for grief. The grief was there, of course, but Hope could discern what others could not. The emotion darkening her eyes was guilt. Guilt that she had sent Andrew storming out of the house the night he'd been killed.

"I'll see you both dead first," he'd told her before he left.

"I'd rather be *dead than stay married to you!"* she'd screamed.

"Careful what you wish for, Hope."

She could understand why Michael, who had admitted a newspaper photograph of Andrew after his death was what had brought him to the Kingsleys in the first place, had clipped her picture from the paper. Everything concerning the Kingsleys would have been of concern to him then, but why had he framed it? Why had this particular photo with the caption, Kingsley's Grieving Widow Leaves Cemetery, made him want to preserve the image behind glass and hide it away?

A dark chill descended over Hope as she stared at the photo. And then, faintly, a sound from outside came to her, sending the chill even deeper. Footsteps in the hallway, coming this way. Slowing as they approached Michael's door.

He'd come back.

Shoving the photo back inside the drawer and easing it closed, Hope glanced around the room, then frantically darted for the closet, staring through the levered doors as her heart pounded inside her. From her vantage, she could see the door to the bedroom open and Michael enter. Without hesitation, he walked toward the bed and was momentarily out of Hope's view. She held her breath. If he was getting ready for bed, he would probably head for the closet. Hardly daring to breathe, Hope glanced around, wondering where she could possibly hide.

But just as she was about to move toward the back of the closet, risking a sound, Michael crossed the room again, and she saw that he was putting his wallet in his pocket. He must have forgotten it when he went out earlier. Hope prayed he would leave again, giving her a chance to escape.

As he moved toward the door, she almost exhaled a long breath of relief. Then his steps slowed and he turned toward the bureau. Hope's heart dropped to her stomach and her palms began to sweat. Had she left one of the drawers open? Had he detected some sign of her search?

She heard one of the drawers open and close, and then Michael walked back into her view, carrying something in his right hand. He sat down on the bed and lifted it in front of him, and only then did Hope realize he held the framed newspaper clipping she'd been looking at only moments earlier.

He stared at the picture of her for a long moment, his expression dark and unfathomable. Then slowly he lifted the frame to his lips and kissed Hope's image.

JAKE OPENED HIS EYES and groaned. The sound came out muffled. A foul-tasting rag had been tied around his mouth, and a jackhammer pounded inside his head. Where the hell was he?

When he tried to lift himself onto his elbows to look around, he realized he couldn't move. Not an inch. He was paralyzed.

Fighting back the panic, Jake tried to analyze the situation rationally. He was lying on his side with his hands tied behind him and his feet bound at the ankles. That was why he couldn't move. The paralysis was only temporary.

Somewhat reassured, he gazed around as best he could. The room was in semidarkness, but he could make out a high, beamed ceiling, a concrete floor, and high racks of barrels and crates and various types of machinery. He was in some sort of warehouse, bound and gagged and waiting for what? His execution? Not if he had anything to say about it.

Tentatively, he tried to wiggle his wrists. Even so slight a movement seemed to tighten the rope. It cut into his skin, and Jake had to resist the urge to struggle, to pull and tear at the rope with every ounce of strength left in him. He knew such an effort would be useless. Whoever had bound him had done a good job of it. Jake would have to be patient, use finesse instead of muscle to loosen the rope.

He worked for what seemed like hours, sweat pouring from his brow, his arms throbbing, the skin beneath the rope raw and burning. The pain inside his head was still almost blinding. Again and again he had to fight back a wave of nausea before he could continue. He had no idea how much time had passed when he finally began to feel the ropes give a little. The hope that rose inside him faded quickly, however, when he heard footsteps approaching him in the darkness.

He lay on his side, eyes closed, and feigned unconsciousness. The footsteps quieted and he could sense someone looming over him. A voice somewhere to his left said, "Is he still out?"

Jake lay perfectly still but his mind raced. He'd heard that voice before. Recently. But…where?

The person standing directly over him said, "Can't tell for sure." Jake recognized that voice, too. It was Benny. "He could be faking it."

"Find out for sure."

Instinctively, Jake braced himself for what was about to come, but even so, when Benny's shoe connected with his ribs, it took all Jake's willpower not to groan. Benny kicked him again, and this time Jake couldn't help but flinch. He hoped neither of them noticed. It was fairly dark in the corner of the warehouse where he lay. As soon as the two thugs moved away, frantically he began to work at the ropes again. He could feel them loosening. Just another knot or maybe two, and he would be free. But did he have that much time?

"He's still out. Guess you hit him pretty hard, Mr.—"

"Don't use my name," the first man interrupted. "How many times do you have to be told that?"

"Sorry."

"You should be sorry. It was a simple matter, what you were told to do. Go to the apartment and get that tape, but you and Carol screwed it up royally."

"Hey, it wasn't our fault. How were we supposed to know some P.I. from Memphis would come sniffing around the place?" Benny mumbled sulkily. "That was all supposed to be taken care of. If you want to blame someone, maybe you should blame *him* for leaving the tape in the apartment to begin with."

Another knot came free. A trickle of sweat rolled down Jake's face.

"You and Carol were supposed to go in behind him and make sure the place was clean. If the boss hadn't noticed the tape was missing, it would have sat in that apartment indefinitely, until who knows who might have stumbled on it. The whole operation could have blown up in our faces, and all because you two idiots forgot to check the VCR. Now we don't know if McClain saw the tape or not, but we can't afford to take the chance. So get rid of him."

"How—"

"Just do it," the man in charge ordered as he started walking away. "Clean up your mess before the boss decides both you and Carol are expendable."

The footsteps faded away, and in a moment, Jake heard a car engine start up, then what sounded like the rumble of an overhead garage door being lifted and lowered again. And then all was silent.

The last knot fell away from Jake's wrists. He wondered how long it would take for the circulation to be restored.

Benny muttered an oath. Intent on taking his irritation out on Jake, he placed another well-aimed kick to Jake's ribs, but this time Jake was ready for him. His hands shot out and he grabbed Benny's leg.

Caught by surprise, Benny lost his balance and fell backward, his skull crashing against the concrete floor. The moment he fell, Jake jerked the gag from his mouth and untied the rope around his ankles.

But Benny was only dazed. After only a few seconds, he struggled to his feet, shaking his head as if to clear the exploding stars behind his eyes. He reached around and drew a gun from the back of his belt, but Jake didn't give him time to aim. Kicking the rope aside, he lunged forward, grabbing Benny around the middle and the gun flew from his hand. Jake dragged him back to the floor, where Jake clearly had the advantage. Kicking a semiconscious man was a lot different from fighting an ex-cop who still kept in shape at the gym. There had been months on end when the only control Jake had over his life was his daily workouts, and he used his muscle now, used every ounce of his strength to pummel his opponent into submission.

Which didn't take much. Benny's glasses were cracked and resting crookedly across his bleeding nose. Jake retrieved the gun from the floor, then grabbed a fistful of Benny's T-shirt and drew him up, aiming the gun at his face.

Benny's heavy breathing sounded almost like sobs. "I give, man. Uncle. Don't kill me."

"Then start talking," Jake said, tightening his finger on the trigger. "Who do you work for?"

"Someone in Memphis," Benny whimpered. "I don't have a name. I swear. The whole organization is hush-hush, real cloak-and-dagger-type stuff. We're only told as much as we need to know."

"What organization?" Jake demanded.

"The Grayson Commission. I connected with them on the Net. It's a political group, very underground. Very into power—"

An explosion somewhere inside the building rattled the windows and rocked the barrels and crates of machinery stacked on the shelves overhead.

Benny's eyes widened in terror. "Jesus. Oh, man. He's wired this place to blow. We have to get out of here!"

No sooner had he said the words than another explosion collapsed some of the shelving in the warehouse, and the barrels and machinery started crashing to the floor all around them. Benny screamed as a wooden crate toppled over them. By the time Jake had pulled himself loose from the splintered wood, Benny was scrambling through the debris.

Jake took off after him, but the roof was caving in now, and the whole warehouse became a giant booby trap. Pallets of equipment stored on upper shelves turned into deadly weapons as they crashed to the floor. Fallen barrels were oozing chemicals, and even a tiny spark might cause the whole place to go up. The fire at the point of the explosions was already starting to spread. Jake had only seconds to find his way out of the warehouse.

In the dim light, amid the chaos, a figure darted through the rubble in front of him. "Freeze!" Jake shouted and took aim, but Benny kept running. Quick as lightning, he shoved open a side door and slid through. Jake raced after him, but by the time he reached the door, Benny had slammed it shut and locked it from the outside.

Jake glanced around, smelling the toxic fumes, feeling the heat from the spreading flames. Shielding his face as best he could, he pointed the gun at the lock and emptied the chamber, hoping the action wouldn't trigger another explosion. But the door swung open and Jake dashed through.

His would-be killer was nowhere to be seen.

Chapter Ten

Jake spent all day Monday showing Eldridge's photograph to any of his neighbors, acquaintances or business associates who could be located. But the interviews generated more questions than answers. Eldridge, it seemed, was something of a loner. None of his neighbors knew him very well, and he had no close friends that Jake was able to turn up. He'd only lived at the Casa del Sol apartments for five months; before that he'd spent a year in a similar group of apartments a few blocks over on Hillcroft.

According to Jake's source at the DMV, Eldridge had changed apartments frequently in the last few years, but that in itself was not all that suspicious. Unlike their Northern counterparts, Southern apartment dwellers were always being lured from their current address by a newer, larger, cheaper apartment down the street. Before Jake had bought his house in Memphis, he'd moved five times in as many years and never once changed his zip code.

The strange thing about Eldridge, though, was people's reaction to his photograph. The few who recognized him did so immediately, but then, without exception, qualified their response with ''But I remember him being taller." Or thinner, shorter, heavier. With darker hair, longer hair, less or more hair. Some even remembered him wearing a mustache.

For the three years Eldridge had been with Richard Crane and Associates, he'd worked almost exclusively from his home, keeping in touch with his office and his clients via phone and E-mail. His supervisor at the brokerage firm had not seen Eldridge in person for several months, but this was not unusual, he assured Jake. Many of their associates were home-based.

On Tuesday morning, Jake drove back to the Casa del Sol apartments, only to find that Eldridge's place had been stripped. Everything was gone, and two uniformed maids were in the process of cleaning, getting the apartment ready for the next tenant.

Jake crossed the parking lot to the leasing office where a bored brunette informed him that Michael Eldridge had phoned her at home late the night before and arranged to have funds wired to the property management's account to settle his lease. By the time she'd arrived for work that morning, the moving van had been waiting to clear out his apartment.

"Did he leave a forwarding address?" Jake asked.

The woman hesitated.

"I'm an old friend of his," he lied. "I think I know where he might have gone. It's a Memphis address, right? He has family there."

The woman pulled a piece of paper from her desk and handed it to Jake. He glanced down. It was the address of the Kingsley mansion.

Jake spent the rest of the day tracking down the foster family Eldridge had been living with at the time of his arrest. With the help of his friend who worked in Juvenile at Houston PD, he finally located the couple, an elderly husband and wife named Donovan. They lived in Cypress, a wooded suburb of Houston, on a street that had once been little more than a country lane but was now surrounded by subdivisions, convenience stores and strip malls.

Their home was a small white wood-frame with an immaculate yard and well-tended flower beds that boasted a variety of blooms Memphis wouldn't see for another few weeks yet.

Mrs. Donovan, a white-haired motherly sort with a whip-thin body and curious gray eyes, came to the door at Jake's knock. Her expression was friendly, but Jake noticed that she made a point of keeping the storm door between them securely locked. Even out in the 'burbs, the darker side of the city couldn't be ignored.

Jake introduced himself, and said, "A friend of mine with the Houston Police Department gave me your name because she thought you might be able to help me out. She said you used to take in foster children back in the sixties and seventies, and there's one in particular I'm interested in. He would have lived here probably around 1974 or '75. His name was Michael Eldridge. Do you remember him?"

Her expression immediately warmed. "Michael! Of course, I remember him. Oh, my goodness, you don't know how many times I've thought about that boy over the years." She turned and called over her shoulder, "Clarence! Come here! There's a friend of Michael's at the door."

Her husband hobbled into view, supporting himself with a cane. He was as thin as his wife, but stoop-shouldered and obviously in poorer health. *"Who?"* he bellowed.

"Michael Eldridge. You remember him. That handsome boy who lived here sometime back in the seventies. Sharp as a tack, that child."

Clarence Donovan's memories didn't seem to be quite so fond. Or else his natural suspicion of strangers was greater than his wife's. He stumped up beside her and glared at Jake through the door. "Who the hell are you?" he demanded.

Jake pulled his identification from his pocket and held it out in front of him. "My name's McClain. I'm a private investigator from Memphis. I'd like to ask you a few questions about Michael Eldridge."

Mrs. Donovan's hand fluttered to her throat. "Oh, dear," she murmured, while Mr. Donovan's glare turned even icier.

"What's he done?" he asked in a tone that implied he just might believe the worst.

Jake hesitated. "May I come in and speak with you for a few minutes?"

"We'll come outside." He motioned Jake away from the door with his cane. "We don't know you from Adam, and I want to make damn sure we're in plain view of plenty of witnesses."

"Good idea." Jake backed away from the door, giving them ample space. He tried to look as non-threatening as possible as he waited for Mr. and Mrs. Donovan to seat themselves in the wicker rockers on the front porch. Jake sat down on the top step of the porch.

"Is Michael all right?" Mrs. Donovan asked anxiously, in a tone that made Jake think they must have been recently in contact.

But when he said as much, Mr. Donovan shook his head. "Haven't seen hide nor hair of that boy since the police took him away that day. Esther remembers all those kids like it was yesterday. We used to have one or two staying here most all the time. Trouble-makers, for the most part. Kids who drifted in and out of the system for years, until they either cleaned up their act or were sent up the river."

"Now, Clarence," Mrs. Donovan said with mild reproach. "You make it sound as if we didn't make a difference in any of those kids' lives. I like to think we did."

Mr. Donovan shrugged, but his expression told Jake he had a differing view of the foster kids who'd passed through their home.

"How long did Eldridge live here?" Jake asked.

"A little more than a year," Esther replied. "He was basically a good boy. Just a little high-spirited."

"High-spirited, hell!" Clarence thundered. "He was a thug and you know it."

Esther glared at him. "Well, was it any wonder? He'd been abandoned when he was five years old. His mother left him in some dirty old Laundromat down by the ship channel and she never came back for him. He was never adopted, either, just shuffled from one foster home to the next, never really having a home or feeling he was wanted. Little wonder he had problems."

"What kind of problems?" Jake asked.

She made a dismissive gesture with one blue-veined hand. "Oh, you know, the usual things boys get into. Skipping school, vandalism, drinking."

"Breaking and entering," Clarence interjected.

"There was just that one time," Esther said, her tone peevish.

"Was that when he was arrested?" Jake asked.

Clarence nodded. "He was fifteen. Just missed being tried as an adult. As it was, some hotshot law firm downtown took his case and he got off with just a stint in juvenile detention. We never saw him after that. Esther here was like a mother to that boy. He was always her favorite. He could charm the damn birds right out of the trees when he had a mind to."

Jake took out the picture of Eldridge and handed it to the Donovans. "Is this the Michael Eldridge you knew?"

Mrs. Donovan took the picture while Mr. Donovan fumbled in his shirt pocket for his glasses, then slipped them on. The two studied the photograph for a long moment, then Mrs. Donovan said, "Oh, my. He's turned out so handsome. And he looks so prosperous."

"He's a stockbroker here in Houston," Jake told them. "He seems to be doing quite well for himself."

"You see, there!" Esther beamed at her husband in triumph. "I knew he would make it. I knew he was someone special."

"If he's turned out so all-fired respectable," Clarence said, eyeing Jake accusingly, "what's your interest in him? He involved in that insider trading scam I been hearing Katie Couric talk about on the *Today* show?"

"No, nothing like that," Jake replied. "Turns out, he may be the long-lost son of a wealthy family in Memphis. I've been hired to check out his background."

"Michael's from a wealthy family?" Esther

clapped her hands together in excitement. "Imagine that, Clarence."

"I'm trying to," Clarence said dryly. "What'd they do, give him away at birth?"

"He may have been kidnapped," Jake told them.

Esther gasped. "How tragic."

"You're sure this is the boy you knew as Michael Eldridge?" Jake nodded toward the picture.

"Oh, yes," Esther said, without equivocation. "That's Michael."

Clarence took the picture from his wife and studied it a little longer. "He was just a kid back then. Fifteen years old. This man's what? Thirty-four, thirty-five? People change in twenty years."

"I'd know him anywhere," Esther declared.

"You don't seem quite as sure," Jake said to Clarence.

The older man rubbed his chin, still staring down at the picture. "Oh, that's him, all right. Only…"

"What?"

"Can't put my finger on it precisely. Something about his eyes…"

JAKE ARRIVED BACK in Memphis just after seven in the evening and drove straight to the Kingsley estate. His father was out, and Jake headed for the shower, brooding over everything that had happened in Houston as he let the hot water sluice over him. Instead of coming home with answers for Hope, he'd returned with more questions.

For instance, what had the blonde been doing at Eldridge's apartment? What was her connection to Andrew Kingsley? Who was the "boss" the two men in the warehouse had referred to? What the hell was the Grayson Commission? And, perhaps most important of all, what had Clarence Donovan seen in Michael Eldridge's photo that had worried him?

As Jake dried off, someone knocked on the front door of the cottage. Slipping on a pair of jeans, he hurried down the stairs to answer it.

Hope stood on the other side.

"I saw you drive up a little while ago. I need to talk to you. May I come in?" She glanced back at the Kingsley mansion. "I don't want anyone to see us."

Jake stood back to let her enter, then closed the door. "Come on out to the kitchen," he said. "I'll get us something to drink."

He started to put his hand on her arm, but she moved away from him, a subtle act, but one he thought he understood. She'd pulled away from him once before, after her father had died. That, too, had been subtle at first. So subtle, Jake hadn't known what was happening until it was too late.

And now she was doing it again. What had happened while he'd been gone?

In the kitchen, he poured them both a glass of iced tea. They sat down at the table, Hope leaving her drink untouched.

"What did you find out in Houston?" she asked.

"Quite a lot, but I'm not sure what any of it means." He gave her a rundown of almost everything, leaving out only a few details he wasn't sure he wanted her to know. Her expression darkened when she heard about the incidents at Eldridge's apartment and the warehouse.

"My God," she whispered. "You could have been killed."

"But I wasn't. So there's no use worrying about it."

"But I got you into this," she protested. "If anything happened to you because of me—"

Her violet gaze fastened on his, and Jake found himself drowning in those eyes. What kind of hold did she have over him? Why couldn't he stay away from her? Why couldn't he forget her? Why couldn't he get on with his life and let Hope do the same?

Because you were meant for each other, a little voice whispered inside him. *You're a part of each other.*

And no matter how much he wanted to deny it, no matter how many times she pulled away from him, Jake knew he would never get Hope out of his system. She lived in his soul. She haunted him.

As if sensing his thoughts, Hope tore her gaze from his and stared down at her glass. "Something happened while you were away."

Her tone sounded ominous. Jake's heart dropped to his stomach. "What?"

She traced a drop of condensation down her glass with her fingertip. "Michael told me that he…has feelings for me."

Did he, by God? Jake managed to remain silent, staring at her inquiringly.

"He said…he said Iris has indicated to him that she would like to see us get together. And she's hinted as much to me, too."

"How do you feel about that?"

Hope drew a long breath. She didn't answer for a moment, and Jake's anger blazed into a bonfire of rage. "Hope, you don't even *know* this guy. Surely to God you're not thinking of taking up with him—"

Hope stared at him in shock. "Of course not! Why would you even think such a thing?"

"He does look like Andrew," Jake said grimly. "And he just may be the next Kingsley heir."

She looked more hurt than angry. "It was never the money with Andrew. Yes, he took me to fancy restaurants and on exotic vacations, bought me beautiful clothes and expensive jewelry. And yes, a part of me enjoyed that way of life. For a while. But it was never enough. It could never take the place of..."

"What?" Jake prompted.

"Of being in love." She stared down at her hands. "Only, I don't think Andrew ever understood that. I don't think he ever gave up the notion that if he lavished me with enough gifts, I might someday fall in love with him."

Jake's gaze impaled her. "And did you?"

"No. I've only been in love once in my life." She lifted her gaze to him. "And Andrew knew that. He couldn't stand that."

Jake wanted more than anything to believe her. How long had he waited to hear those words? But something inside him wouldn't let him give voice to his emotions. Not yet. He ran a hand through his damp hair. "Yeah, well, knowing the woman you love is in love with someone else is pretty damn hard to take for anyone." He felt a flash of unexpected sympathy for Andrew Kingsley.

"It wasn't just that," Hope said. "I sometimes think it had more to do with *you* than it did with me. Because *you* were the man I had fallen in love with. Because *you* had something he didn't. He hated you, Jake. It sometimes scared me how much he hated you."

"He wasn't exactly on my Top Ten list, either," Jake said. "But what does any of this have to do with Michael Eldridge's feelings for you?"

"Maybe nothing," Hope said. "Maybe...everything."

"You'd better explain that."

"I hardly know where to start." She got up and paced to the kitchen window, staring out at the tiny backyard Jake's father had turned into his own private garden. "You'll think I've lost my mind."

"Why don't you try me?"

She turned, toying with the pearl button at the top of her blue sweater. "You've seen him for yourself, Jake. You know how much he looks like Andrew. How much he *acts* like Andrew."

A tiny buzzing in Jake's ears sounded a warning, but he ignored it. He had to hear this, no matter how much it might hurt. "Go on."

"If he really is *Adam* Kingsley, then that explains why he looks so much like Andrew. Identical twins, even raised apart, would still bear a strong resemblance to each other, might even look exactly like each other. But...that doesn't explain his mannerisms. The reason why he walks like Andrew, talks like Andrew. Uses the same words Andrew would use..." She drew a long breath. "It doesn't explain the way he looks at me."

"You think he *is* Andrew," Jake said, almost accusingly.

Hope closed her eyes briefly. "I know it's crazy. But there's something about him...something that sends cold chills through me every time I look at him. Every time he looks at me. Jake, what if Andrew didn't die in that car crash—"

He crossed the distance between them in two strides and took hold of her arms, forcing her to face him. "Andrew is dead, Hope. He's dead."

"But I didn't see his body, and neither did you. You said yourself there wasn't an autopsy—"

"Plenty of people saw Andrew dead. The Shepherd authorities, the EMTs, doctors and nurses at the hospital. You said Victor Northrup identified the body."

This last seemed to jolt her. Her gaze shot back up to his. He saw a glimmer of something he couldn't identify in her eyes. "That still doesn't explain the picture."

"What picture?"

"The one he has in his room...of me."

Jake realized he still held her arms and that his grip had tightened. He forced his hands to drop to his sides. "What were you doing in Eldridge's room?"

She glanced up at him. "I went there to search it."

"You *what?*" He glared at her incredulously. "I don't have to tell you how stupid that was, do I? Hope, for all we know, this man is dangerous. A homicidal maniac or worse."

She laughed shakily. "What could be worse than a homicidal maniac?"

"Believe me, you don't want to know. Just what the hell were you thinking?"

"I thought I might find a clue to his real identity, okay?" She glared up at him defiantly. "Something that might help us in the investigation. What I found was a picture of me. A newspaper clipping of me leaving the cemetery after Andrew's burial. He...oh, God, Jake. He'd *framed* it." The last traces of defiance drained from her face, and what Jake saw was a woman very much afraid. Not for her life, he suspected, but for her peace of mind.

"I found it in his drawer, under some socks. Then I heard him coming back. He was right outside the door before I realized it. I shoved the picture back inside the drawer and hid in the closet." When Jake would have said something else, she held up her hand. "It's okay, he didn't find me. He'd only come back because he'd forgotten his wallet. But before he left again, he went over to the bureau and took out the picture. I saw him..." She faltered, glancing away, not quite able to meet Jake's eyes. "I saw him kiss my picture," she finished in a whisper.

Something closed over Jake's heart. A knot of fear. A fist of rage. *I'll kill him,* he thought. *I'll kill him before I'll let him touch you.*

"What did you do?" he asked with as much calm as he could muster.

Hope shrugged. "Nothing. I just felt sick. I waited until he'd left, and then I went back to my room as fast as I could." She paused again, as if summoning her own calm. "What do you make of all this?"

"I don't know." The image of Hope's face against Eldridge's lips—Andrew's lips—was something Jake couldn't quite dispel. He took a few steps away from her, staring out at the gathering darkness in his father's backyard. "Was your wedding videotaped?"

He wasn't looking at her, but he could sense her shock and confusion at his question. "Why?"

"Just answer the question, and then I'll explain."

"Yes, it was. In fact, it caused a big row between Andrew and Iris. She said videotaping such a sacred ceremony was vulgar, but Andrew insisted. He said he wanted to capture the happiest moment of our lives on tape so that years later, we could share it with our children. He assured Iris he would hire a professional, someone who would blend in with the guests and we'd hardly know he was there.''

"Did you ever see the tape?"

Hope shook her head. "I asked Andrew about it a few times, but he said it was too soon to look at it. It would be better if we waited until some sort of milestone in our marriage, like our tenth anniversary. By then, of course, neither of us cared to see it. At least, I didn't." She paused. "Jake, what's this about?"

He hadn't wanted to tell her about the videotape in Eldridge's VCR, but now he didn't have a choice. She had to know what she was dealing with here. When he explained, the color drained from her face. "If he isn't Andrew, how did he get that tape?"

"Any number of ways," Jake said. "Whoever Andrew hired to tape the wedding could have kept a copy for himself, thinking he could peddle it to the tabloids. I don't know how it might have come into Eldridge's possession, but I do know this. There *is* a Michael Eldridge. I talked to too many people in Houston who knew him.''

She still didn't look convinced. "If he is Michael Eldridge, nothing more than a stranger, why would he have that tape and that picture of me?"

Jake shrugged. The obvious answer wasn't one he much cared to explore. "He must have studied the Kingsleys for some time, figuring out the best way to approach Iris. Maybe he became...interested in you in the process." He would have said *fixated. Obsessed.* But then he might have had to explore his own psyche a little too closely.

"What about the blonde?" Hope asked, changing the subject so quickly, Jake knew she was have trouble dealing with the explanation as well.

"She is definitely a connection between Eldridge and Andrew," Jake said. "It was no coincidence she was at Eldridge's door. Someone sent her there for that videotape. And she was with Andrew the night he died."

"Are you implying she may have had something to do with the car crash? That Andrew's death—"

"May have been murder," Jake finished bluntly.

"Dear God." He didn't think her face could go any whiter; but for a moment, he thought she might actually pass out. He reached for her, but Hope waved away his hand. It seemed a point of pride with her that she handle this, that she not succumb to her fear. That she not depend on *him* for strength.

"We talked about this before." He shoved his hands into the pockets of his jeans. "I've never thought Eldridge was working alone, and now we know for sure there are at least four other people involved in this thing. The blonde, the two men in the warehouse, and the 'boss' they talked about. And, of course, something called the Grayson Commission."

"You told me once that an attorney in Victor Northrup's firm was from Houston, that he'd defended Michael when he was a teenager. You thought he might have been the one to mention to Victor or to Jeremy that he had a client who looked like Andrew. Do you remember that?"

"Yeah. And I still say that's a likely possibility," Jake said.

"There was one other person he might have mentioned the look-alike to."

Jake glanced at her warily. There was something in her tone he didn't like. "Who?"

Her gaze met his. "Andrew. Supposing the attorney saw Andrew in Victor's office and told him how much he looked like his Houston client? Supposing Andrew is the one who filed that tidbit away until one day when he was desperate, fearing for his life from Simon Pratt. What if he thought he could switch places with Michael Eldridge so that Pratt couldn't find him? Then by coming here and pretending to be *Adam,* he could still be the Kingsley heir. He could still live in luxury and still have Iris's adoration. And he might even be able to win me back. That would explain the picture and the videotape. That would explain so many things," she finished softly.

Jake's gaze hardened on her. "How far are you willing to take this, Hope?"

"What do you mean?"

"A body was recovered from that crash. If it was Andrew's double, then someone had to have made the switch. Someone had to have killed the real Michael Eldridge. Do you believe Andrew capable of murder?"

"I'll see you both dead first."

Andrew's words echoed through Hope's mind. An empty threat, she'd thought at the time; but the look in his eyes had come back to haunt her. He would have done anything to keep her away from Jake. Hope had no doubt about that. Rage and obsession were powerful motivators, but Andrew had an even stronger one. The instinct for survival. If Simon Pratt had been closing in, how far would Andrew have gone to save himself? To win the ultimate game?

She could almost hear him laughing at them now.

The image was so strong she had to fight the childish inclination to cover her ears with her hands.

"The scenario you've just outlined would have taken an incredible amount of planning to pull off," Jake said. "Andrew couldn't have done it alone. Someone with money and clout would have had to pull a lot of strings, bribe a lot of people, and that would make the risk of discovery fairly high. Do you know anyone like that, Hope?"

She knew who he was getting at. Iris. The same thought had even crossed Hope's mind. But the status and power of the Kingsley name meant everything to Iris, maybe even more than the family itself. Would she have been willing to risk losing all that she held dear to help her grandson pull off such an elaborate hoax?

She'd adored Andrew, no question. And as fond as Hope was of Iris, she had no delusions about the Kingsley matriarch. Hope knew Iris had done things in her life that Hope herself probably wouldn't approve of, might even find shocking. But there was no way Iris would ever be a party to murder. No matter what else she might have done.

"What other choices do we have?" she asked.

"There's always good ol' Jeremy and Mommy Dearest," Jake said. "Although I haven't ruled out Northrup. There's something about that man I don't trust, other than the fact that he's Iris's oldest and dearest friend. But regardless of who's behind this scheme, it's obvious that with Andrew out of the way, an impostor would have a much greater chance of worming his way into Iris's affections."

"Pamela's greedy and ambitious, and God knows, Jeremy is…strange enough. And I'll admit Victor is a little on the slick side. But to commit murder. To kill Andrew in cold blood..." She shuddered.

"There is another possibility," Jake said. "Maybe Michael Eldridge really is Adam Kingsley. And he already knows it."

"But then where would the blonde come in? She's the connection between Michael and Andrew. You think she may have had something to do with Andrew's death. But if Michael knows he's the real Adam Kingsley, why would he have his own brother killed?"

"Do the math, Hope. One heir would inherit twice as much money as two."

Even though the evening was warm, Hope shivered. Somehow the notion of Adam Kingsley deliberately plotting to murder his identical twin—a brother he didn't even know—for the Kingsley fortune was more chilling than anything they'd discussed so far.

"I want you to stay away from him, Hope," Jake warned, as if reading her mind. "Get out of that house. Now. Tonight. Go to your mother's. Wherever. But don't go back there."

"I can't do that," Hope said, even as she wished desperately to do exactly as Jake instructed.

"Why the hell not?"

"Because if he is Adam, if he killed his own brother to become the Kingsley heir, then what's preventing him from killing Iris, so that the money becomes his immediately?"

"Iris isn't my primary concern at the moment," Jake replied. "Damn it, Hope, be reasonable."

"I am being reasonable. She's an old woman, Jake. Far more vulnerable than she wants to admit. Edward is completely useless, and Pamela and Jeremy... For all we know, they're in on this thing. I can't leave her to the wolves. You wouldn't be able to, either.''

Jake scowled as he glanced out into the darkness. "Okay. I guess you're right. But for God's sake, be careful. If you feel even a hint of danger, promise me you'll get the hell out of there. Don't try to take care of this yourself. Whoever these people are, they may already have killed once. I don't think they'd hesitate to do so again.''

JAKE WALKED HOPE to the fringes of the Kingsley gardens, not daring to go any farther for fear they'd be seen together. The less anyone suspected Hope's involvement in Jake's investigation into Eldridge's background, the safer she would be. And at the moment, Hope's safety was all Jake cared about.

The light had faded rapidly, but the moon was already up, a waning half-globe against a black velvet sky sprinkled with stars. They paused near a flowering bush that Jake couldn't name, but the fragrance was as familiar as a lover's perfume.

He stared down into Hope's upturned face and thought again how extraordinarily beautiful she was. How much he wanted to hold her. Keep her safe. Keep her all to himself.

But tonight there was someone else in the garden with them. An invisible presence that kept them apart. That made Hope pull away from him even when he knew that she wanted him, too.

Andrew is dead, goddamn it.

But the doubt was still there in Hope's eyes. And as long as she believed there was a chance her husband remained alive, Andrew would keep on winning. He would succeed in keeping them apart.

"I'd better go," she said softly. "Someone might see us."

When she would have turned away, Jake caught her arm and pulled her back to him. "Hope," he said urgently. "Andrew *is* dead. You do know that, don't you?"

She hesitated, a part of her resisting his touch even as her eyes told him what he wanted to know. "That's what I keep telling myself. But what if he's not, Jake? What if he's still alive? What if I'm still his wife?"

"It wouldn't make a damned bit of difference to me," Jake said darkly.

"But it would to me. And it certainly would to Andrew."

HOPE SLIPPED THROUGH the gardens, trying to keep to the shadows, so that anyone looking out from one of the rear windows of the mansion wouldn't see her returning from the direction of the gardener's cottage. But as she skirted the edge of the pool, someone rose from one of the lounges. She gasped, her hand darting to her throat.

Michael Eldridge, dressed in dark trousers and a collarless dark shirt that made him blend with the night, walked slowly toward her. He'd lit a fire in the brick hearth near the end of the pool, and the flickering flames reflected in his eyes and cast dark shadows across his face, making him look almost savage. Jake's warning echoed in Hope's ears.

She laughed nervously. "Michael, you startled me. I wasn't expecting to see anyone out here."

He took another step toward her, and Hope had to

fight the urge to turn and flee. A myriad of possibilities flashed through her mind—none of them comforting. Michael Eldridge/devious impostor. Michael Eldridge/the real Adam Kingsley. Michael Eldridge/Andrew.

Michael Eldridge/murderer.

"I've been waiting for you," he said.

Something in his tone sent a shiver of fear down Hope's spine. She glanced up at him, trying to keep her expression from revealing her emotions. "Why?"

"I heard from my boss down in Houston today. He said a private investigator from Memphis came around asking questions about me. You wouldn't happen to know anything about that, would you?"

"Why would I know?"

"Let's don't play games." His voice hardened. "Iris made her wishes clear to the family. She didn't want me investigated. What do you think she would do if she found out you'd hired McClain, of all people, to snoop around in my business?"

Hope forced a bravado into her tone she was far from feeling. "What makes you think *I* hired him? I imagine there are a lot of people who would like to know who you really are."

"The DNA tests results will be back soon. They'll tell you everything about me you need to know."

"And if it turns out you aren't Adam Kingsley?" Hope met his gaze without wavering. "Will you go back to Houston? Disappear from Iris's life?"

"If that's what she wants." He gazed down at her with a smile that sent a chill through Hope's heart. "But Iris has become quite attached to me, you know. She has high hopes for my future. And for yours."

"You can leave me out of this," Hope said. "Regardless of who you are, I'm not part of the equation. As soon as everything's settled, I intend to find a place of my own.''

"You really think it'll be that easy? Just pack up and walk out, and leave the past behind you?'' The flames in the hearth had died down, leaving his face more in shadow. "Life is rarely that simple, Hope. Iris has a way of getting what she wants. Or so I've been told.''

"That may be true,'' Hope replied. "But she can't force me to stay here against my will. No one can do that.''

"There are always more subtle ways of getting what we want.'' He reached out and grasped her arms with his hands, pulling her toward him so quickly, Hope had no time to resist. His mouth came down on hers, hot, fierce and possessive. His tongue tried to part her lips, but Hope shoved him away, resisting the urge to bring her knee up between his legs as her father had taught her to do to ward off an attacker.

Instead she pulled away from him, wiping the back of her hand across her mouth. "Don't ever do that again,'' she warned.

"You're right.'' His tone was surprisingly contrite. "That wasn't very subtle. I apologize.''

Hope had expected him to laugh in her face or try to grab her again, but instead he turned and walked back to the hearth, holding his hands over the flames.

She studied his face in the flickering light, wondering who he really was. Wondering if the man standing before her was capable of murder. And if she had just provoked him.

As if reading her thoughts, he looked up, meeting her gaze in the firelight. "I am sorry, Hope. I didn't mean to frighten you. Believe it or not, that's the last thing I want to do.''

His expression held genuine regret, and his eyes were shadowed with something that looked very much like pain. In that instant, Hope thought he had never looked more like Andrew.

Chapter Eleven

Jake spent a restless night, tossing and turning and worrying about Hope being in that house with Michael Eldridge, a man they knew very little about. A man who may have killed her husband. It sent chills down Jake's back to think of that same man kissing her picture. Wanting her. Perhaps even touching her...

Jake couldn't get the images out of his mind, and when morning finally came, he got out of bed with more resolve than he'd ever had. He would find out everything there was to know about Michael Eldridge. The sooner they knew who and what they were dealing with, the sooner he could get Hope away from that house. Away from those memories...

But would he ever really be able to do that? he asked himself grimly as he drove to his office later that morning. Andrew had been an important part of Hope's life for ten years. She had been with Andrew a lot longer than she'd been with Jake. Was what he and Hope once shared, what they shared now, strong enough to vanquish a dead husband who still haunted her dreams?

He knew she no longer loved Andrew—might

never have really loved him. But as long as she thought there was a possibility he remained alive, she would never give her feelings for Jake a chance. She would suppress them as she had done last night. As she had done ten years ago when she broke off their engagement.

As Jake saw it, he could do one of two things. He could walk away as he'd done ten years ago, his pride intact, or he could fight for her this time. And the only way he knew how to do that was to find out the truth about Michael Eldridge. It always came back to that.

Because you can't fight an enemy you know nothing about.

Sitting down at his computer, Jake logged on to the Internet, using his favorite search engine to look for the term "Grayson Commission," one of the few pieces of information he'd been able to glean from Benny before all hell had broken loose in the warehouse. Having no success at first, Jake thought the guy must have made the whole thing up, or else all references to the Grayson Commission were so obscure or so well hidden, one had to know exactly where to look to find them.

But finally he got a hit. The Grayson Commission came up in a listing for political groups, and following the trail, Jake quickly realized the association. It was on the fringe, out of the mainstream. He jumped to one of the chat rooms where he listened in on a discussion concerning Ruby Ridge and Waco. As soon as he'd entered the room, "Mac," the ID he used on the Internet, appeared in a corner of the screen. After a few minutes, someone calling himself "Nukum" addressed him.

Nukum: Who the hell are you?

Mac: A curious bystander. I'm interested in a group called the Grayson Commission. Ever heard of it?

Nukum: Yeah, but I've never heard of you. What are you doing in here?

Mac: It's a free country, last I heard.

Nukum: Not for long, pal.

Mac: So you don't know anything about the Grayson Commission.

Nukum: I didn't say that. As a matter of fact, I've been studying this group for a long time.

Mac: Then you ought to be able to help me out here.

Nukum: Maybe. What's your angle? Are you into radical politics?

Mac: I know who the Freemen are.

Nukum: Man, you are way off. The Grayson Commission is full of subversives, all right, but they work from inside the system. Like the Trilateral Commission, only not so global.

Mac: What's their agenda?

Nukum: To place handpicked officials in positions of power, both locally and nationally, in order to establish an independent base of power for the elite few, that is, their own membership. In other words, they're into making money, man. Big time.

Mac: You seem to know all about this group. Are you a member?

Nukum: I don't know all about it. No one does.

Mac: I hear it's pretty hush-hush.

Nukum: Right up there with Area 51.

Mac: Who are some of the members?
Nukum: You're better off not knowing.
Mac: Why's that?

There was a pause.

Nukum: Because if you knew that, you'd be
dead.

HOPE AGREED TO MEET Jake for lunch at the Rendezvous, a basement restaurant downtown world-
renowned for its ribs. They were both late arriving,
so most of the lunch crowd had already cleared out
by the time they chose a corner table and placed their
orders.

Hope was glad that she'd taken the time to change
from the white linen dress she'd been wearing earlier
into jeans and a dark blue top. She hadn't eaten here
in years, but it hadn't changed at all. Even though a
lot of businessmen lunched at the Rendezvous, the
atmosphere was still very casual, and jeans were definitely more practical for eating ribs than a white linen
dress.

Jake ordered a pitcher of beer and filled their mugs
when it arrived. After the waitress had departed, he
remained silent for a moment, then glanced up at her.
"We may be into something a lot heavier than either
of us realized."

"What do you mean?" Hope asked, alarmed by
his tone. Jake always had a tendency to look intense,
but she could tell something was bothering him today,
something—as he said—heavy.

He rubbed at a spot over his eyebrow, buying himself some time, she thought, because he wasn't sure where to start. Or how she would take it.

"Do you remember I told you that the guy in the warehouse in Houston mentioned an organization called the Grayson Commission? He implied that he worked for them. He also said that he'd hooked up with this group over the Internet."

"Yes, but you thought he may have made the whole thing up, just to throw you off track."

"But he didn't," Jake said. "There is something called the Grayson Commission. At least, people on the Net seem to know about it, and it sounds like a pretty dark little group, from what I could gather. Businessmen, politicians, even some criminal types in some sort of unholy, moneymaking alliance to get their own people elected to public office, so that they can change or adapt policy to the benefit of their own membership."

Hope grimaced. "Sounds like the plot of a really bad made-for-TV movie."

"Yeah," Jake agreed. "Except this is real life. And you and I may have landed right smack in the middle of it." He paused, taking a long swig of beer. "I think we've gone about this all wrong, Hope. We've been operating on the assumption that Michael Eldridge—and whoever is backing him—is in this for the money. But what if the Kingsley legacy they're really after is power? Political clout? Think about it for a minute. If this organization has somehow managed to recruit a Kingsley look-alike who is good enough to convince Iris he's her long-lost grandson, there's no telling how far he could go with her help. To the governor's mansion. Capitol Hill. Maybe even the White House."

"Wait a minute," Hope said, trying to catch her breath. "You're moving way too fast for me."

"Sorry." Excitement gleamed in Jake's eyes. "But all the possibilities have been going around in my head all morning. I think we may be on to something really big here."

"Let's just take one thing at a time," Hope suggested. "Supposing this Grayson Commission, if it really does even exist, *is* after the Kingsley power and political expertise with an eye toward getting Michael elected to public office—with Iris's help. If they're not after the money, why kill Andrew?"

Jake shrugged. "It's like I said last night. With Andrew out of the picture, Eldridge had a better shot of being accepted by Iris. There she was, grieving for her dead grandson when out of the blue, her other grandson who'd disappeared thirty-one years ago—had even been thought dead for most of that time—appears on her doorstep, looking for all the world like the grandson she just lost. If Andrew had still been alive, do you think she would have welcomed Eldridge into her home without questions? Without reservations? Without an *investigation?* I don't think so. Not the Iris Kingsley I remember."

"All right," Hope conceded. "I guess I can buy all that. But if the Grayson Commission is as powerful as you say and they're ultimately after the Kingsleys' political pull, then why didn't they try to recruit Andrew? Wouldn't that have been easier than trying to plant an impostor inside the family?"

"For all we know, they may have approached him at some time or other, but Andrew never had any political ambitions, did he, Hope?"

In fact, he'd had very few ambitions, period, Hope

reflected, but somehow, admitting it to Jake would seem disloyal to Andrew's memory. He'd been her husband, after all, even if at times loyalty had not been a two-way street. But Hope had taken her vows seriously. The idea of divorce had torn at her; still tore at her now when she remembered the look on Andrew's face the night he'd stormed out of the house.

Guilt was a funny thing. She'd been entertaining thoughts for days now that Andrew might still be alive, might be deceiving her in just about the worst way possible, that he might even be willing to commit murder to pull off that deception, and yet she still felt twinges of guilt that she hadn't been able to make her marriage work. Guilt that she had feelings—powerful feelings—for a man her husband had detested.

"If all this is true," she said slowly, "then we're no longer talking about someone in the family, or even close to the family, being responsible for Michael Eldridge's arrival in Memphis. The people you're talking about are strangers."

"I'm not so sure about that," Jake said, warming to the subject. He was completely in his element, Hope thought. Solving life-and-death riddles as if they were of no more consequence than the crossword puzzle in the Sunday paper. "I keep coming back to Pamela and Jeremy. For my money, they seem to have the most to gain. Jeremy especially. Like you said, he doesn't have a prayer of being Iris's heir, and from everything you've told me, I doubt she'd be willing to back him in the political arena, either."

"You're right about that," Hope replied.

"Think how it's been for him, growing up in that house, knowing he'd never get his hands on the

Kingsley fortune and he'd never have access to the Kingsley power. Power that Andrew so carelessly threw away. I would imagine a lot of resentment would have been built up over the years, and I can see how he might easily have been recruited by an organization like the Grayson Commission. They could have convinced him that by helping Michael Eldridge pose as Adam, Jeremy would not only gain access to the fortune denied him all these years, but when and if Eldridge came into political prominence, Jeremy would be right there calling the shots from the sidelines, gaining vicarious power through his Kingsley look-alike.''

"This still sounds pretty far-fetched to me," Hope said. "But if the Grayson Commission is behind everything that's happened, there's another connection we haven't yet explored. Remember the night Pratt had us taken to his compound in Shepherd? He said that Jonas Thorpe had come to him by way of Houston.''

Jake glanced up at her, a spark of admiration in his eyes. "I'd forgotten about that. But you're right. We can't discount Simon Pratt in all this. According to what I read on the Net, organized crime is heavily involved in the Grayson Commission. And Pratt definitely had a connection to the Kingsleys through Andrew.'' Jake refilled their mugs from the pitcher of beer while they waited for their food. "There's also another person we haven't discussed.''

Hope took a sip of her beer. "Who?"

"Iris.''

She gazed at him in shock. "You can't seriously think she'd be involved with an organization like the Grayson Commission. Why would she?''

Jake shrugged again. "For power, what else? From all I've ever heard about Iris Kingsley, that's what she's always craved more than anything else. She must have been pretty bummed out when Edward, her only son, went against her wishes and decided not to run for more than two terms as governor."

Hope winced. "Livid was more like it, according to Andrew. He once told me that after Edward made his decision, Iris didn't speak to him for almost two years, even though they were living in the same house. She blamed Pamela for Edward's downfall, and generally made everyone's life miserable. Then one day, she just sort of snapped out of her bitterness and started pinning all her hopes on Andrew."

"Who, as you've pointed out, had absolutely no political aspirations. She must have seen the end of the Kingsley dynasty coming for a long time, but then a man claiming to be Adam turns up and suddenly there's a light at the end of the tunnel."

"But what if he's not Adam?" Hope asked.

"Maybe it doesn't matter to her. Maybe the fact that he looks like Andrew is enough. As long as the Kingsley power is restored and the dynasty continued, maybe it doesn't matter to her who this man is. Think about it for a minute, Hope. Why didn't she want him investigated?"

"What you say makes a certain kind of twisted sense," Hope admitted. "But, Jake, there's no way she would have had anything to do with Andrew's death. You have to know that."

"And I'll concede that point. Reluctantly," Jake said, but Hope could see how much he relished the possibility that Iris was somehow involved in all this. "But what if the Grayson Commission didn't contact her until after Andrew's death, when she was vulnerable and lonely and needed something to focus on other than her grief? Iris Kingsley is a very complex woman, Hope. I don't think we can afford to lose sight of how powerful she is, or how much that power means to her.''

"Jake—''

"I know how you feel about her.'' He stared at her across the table. "I know she's always been good to you, and you feel a certain amount of loyalty to her. I can understand that. But we have to keep an open mind. We have to consider all the possibilities. I thought that's why you hired me. To find out the truth about Eldridge, no matter where that truth leads me.''

"I did. And you're right. We do have to consider all the possibilities. Only—''

"Only what?''

She glanced at him accusingly. "Do you have to enjoy all this quite so much?''

He leaned across the table. "Admit it. You like it, too. It's fun being part of the hunt.''

"You call being hit over the head and tied up in a burning warehouse fun?'' she demanded.

"It has its moments.'' He sat back and eyed her with amusement. "You know, you've got a real flair for police work, Hope. Who would have thought it?''

She would have retorted that she certainly did not have a flair for police work, that she still had nightmares about Pratt's Dobermans chasing them through the woods, but just then the platters of food arrived, along with a stack of paper napkins.

The succulent aroma of barbecued pork ribs stirred hunger pangs in Hope. After the serious nature of their discussion, she was surprised to find she even had an appetite, but she and Jake both attacked their meals with gusto.

When they were finished, they had not only an alarming pile of bones stacked beside their plates, but an equal number of napkins. Eating ribs was a messy business, and Hope had enjoyed every minute of it.

"I'm stuffed," she groaned. "I can't believe I ate so much."

"You can afford it." Jake gave her an appreciative glance. "I've been thinking you're a little on the skinny side."

"Oh, really? I'm the exact same size I was when I first met you," she informed him. "And I don't recall any complaints back then."

Suddenly, in the midst of their playful sparring, a memory of something Jake had said to her the first time they'd made love shot through Hope. *"You're so perfect,"* he whispered. *"Everywhere I touch. Here."* He kissed her neck. *"Here."* His hand cupped her breast. *"Here."* His fingers skimmed down her stomach. *"And here..."*

Hope's eyes lifted to meet Jake's, and in that instant, she knew he was experiencing the very same memory. The remembered sensations wove a bond of intimacy between them, making Hope wonder what it would be like to be in Jake's arms now, having him explore all the erotic places he'd once known so well.

I've missed you, she thought suddenly, with an intensity that stole her breath away. *God, how I've missed you.*

"Mrs. Kingsley?" said a voice at Hope's side.

Reluctantly Hope tore her gaze from Jake's and glanced up. The woman was an acquaintance whose name Hope couldn't recall, but she remembered having met her at a dinner party Iris had given before Andrew died.

"I thought that was you," the woman said with a satisfied smile. "I was so sorry to hear about Andrew. What an awful time you must have had."

"Thank you," Hope murmured, resenting the intrusion in spite of herself.

The woman threw Jake a curious glance. "He was so handsome," she said almost pointedly, as if she'd somehow sensed the heat flashing between him and Hope. "Such a charmer. I can't imagine how much you must miss him."

"No," Hope replied. "You really can't."

"Well, it was good to see you again," the woman said reluctantly, as if she wasn't quite ready to leave. As if she might retrieve a bit of juicy gossip if she hung around long enough. "Please give Iris my regards."

Finally she drifted away, leaving Hope and Jake alone, but the moment of intimacy was gone, shattered once again by the intrusion of Andrew's ghost.

HOPE WAS INFORMED as soon as she got home that Iris wanted to see her. She went straight up and knocked on Iris's door, then entered when she heard Iris call out to her.

Dressed in a beaded, royal purple evening gown and seated arrow-straight on her favorite chair in her sitting room, Iris looked as queenly as Hope had ever seen her. She beckoned to Hope with a hand heavily bejeweled in diamonds and amethysts, looking for all the world like a woman who would be presiding over a state dinner in a few hours rather than the family's evening meal.

"You look wonderful," Hope said. "What's the occasion?"

"We'll get to that in a moment." She motioned Hope to the settee across from her and waited until Hope had settled herself before she spoke again. "There is something quite important I wish to discuss with you, but first, tell me what you've been up to, my dear. I haven't seen much of you lately. How have you been occupying yourself?"

An alarm sounded inside Hope. Had Michael told Iris about her and Jake's investigation? Possibilities flitted through Hope's mind. Should she pretend ignorance? Flat-out deny it? What would Jake do?

Then it came to Hope. Jake would try to turn the situation to his advantage. He would try to gather as much information as he could, maybe even go on the offensive and use the element of surprise to observe Iris's reaction.

"You have a flair for police work, Hope."

Let's hope you're right, she thought.

She glanced up at Iris and smiled. "Actually, I've been doing a bit of research lately. There's an organization I saw mentioned somewhere—I don't remember exactly where—that's aroused my curiosity. I've been trying to learn more about it."

"What organization is that, my dear?"

"An underground political group called the Grayson Commission. Have you ever heard of it?"

Something flashed in Iris's eyes, a glint of recognition before she quickly suppressed it with a look of mild curiosity. "I don't believe so. But then, the Kingsleys have never been interested in subversive movements. Our political views are very open and straightforward, and for the most part, in tune with

mainstream America. Tell me something, my dear."
Her eyes glittered like sapphires as she eyed Hope for
a long, silent moment. "Is this Grayson Commission
something Jake McClain dug up for you?"

Hope's heart thudded against her chest. So much
for the offensive. She should have known better than
to try to match wits with Iris Kingsley. "How long
have you known?"

"That you'd hired Jake to investigate Michael?"
Iris's smile was as cool as frostbite. "Almost from
the beginning. You didn't really think you could keep
it from me, did you?"

Hope rubbed a temple with her fingertips. "Look,
I'm sorry. I know I shouldn't have gone behind your
back like that, but I felt it was something I had to do.
I was worried about you. I still am. But if you want
me to move out, just say the word. I'll understand."

Hope realized a part of her wanted desperately for
Iris to say, *"Yes, that's exactly what I want. Pack
your bags, Hope, and don't come back."* Then her
obligation to Andrew's grandmother would be alle-
viated. She could leave with a clear conscience. But
instead, Iris gazed at her fondly, the frost melting
from her smile. "My dear, that is the last thing I want.
You are a part of this family, Hope. You're a Kingsley. Don't ever forget that."

"But…you aren't angry with me?"

"Angry? For caring whether a grief-stricken old
woman might be duped by a devious impostor?"
Iris's expression hardened. "You are the only member of this family who had enough guts to go against
my wishes and hire an investigator. And while I may
not agree with your choice, I can't quibble with your
motives. Angry with you? If anything, my admiration

for you has grown. As has my gratitude. You did exactly what I would have done in your place."

This was going too well, Hope thought uneasily. Iris was up to something.

"Well, now that it's all out in the open," Iris said briskly, smoothing an invisible wrinkle from the skirt of her gown, "tell me, what has Jake learned about our Michael?"

"Several things, actually," Hope answered vaguely, uncertain how much she wanted to reveal to Iris at this point. She remembered Jake's warning that they mustn't discount Iris's power or her willingness to use it.

Iris toyed with a diamond ring on her finger. "Has he found anything that proves Michael is anyone other than who he claims to be?"

"No," Hope admitted reluctantly.

"Anything that proves he is not Adam?"

"No."

Iris smiled. "Then I don't want to know anything else. You've told me all I need to know. And tonight, all *your* questions will be answered."

"What do you mean?" Hope demanded, a feeling of dread slipping over her.

Iris's eyes sparkled with undisguised excitement. "Victor called. The DNA tests are back. He will announce the results after dinner tonight. In a few short hours, everyone will know, as I already do, that Michael really is a Kingsley. He *is* my grandson."

Chapter Twelve

The stage was set for drama, Hope decided as she descended the stairs later that evening. Iris had put out the word that dinner would be a formal affair and everyone was to dress accordingly. Hope had chosen a lavender Vera Wang, very simply but exquisitely cut, that she'd worn only once before. She'd pulled her hair back into a French knot and secured it with a diamond clasp, her only adornment other than the diamond studs in her earlobes.

The Kingsley gardens and hothouses had been raided to provide dozens of lavish floral arrangements. The sweet, heady aroma of spring flowers filled the air, contrasting sharply with the dark feeling of dread that had been growing inside Hope since Iris's announcement earlier.

Tonight they would find out who Michael Eldridge really was.

Hope felt a flutter of apprehension in her stomach. How would the revelation affect her? she wondered. Or would it?

She wished that Jake could be there with her when she heard the news, but that was impossible. Jake would never be invited into the Kingsley home, and even if he was, he would be expected to use the rear entrance. Hope had the strongest desire to go through that back door herself, walk through the gardens to the cottage and find Jake. Ask him to take her away from all this—and she would never look back.

But she knew she couldn't do that. For her own peace of mind, she had to see this thing through. With any luck, she would be leaving this house in the near future. And she wouldn't be coming back.

As usual, everyone had gathered in the library for predinner cocktails. Hope wavered in the doorway, using the opportunity to study those already present. Iris, of course, she'd seen earlier, but the effect of her gown and jewels had not faded. The soft lighting in the library caught the beading of her dress and the ornate diamond-and-amethyst necklace at her throat, casting a rich glow over her features.

Michael was at her side, as attentive and solicitous as always and looking as if he had been born to wear the tuxedo that fit his trim physique to perfection.

Seated on Iris's other side was Victor Northrup, his silver hair gleaming in the soft light, his formal attire unmistakably Armani.

Edward sat across from them, also formally dressed, but a sad parody of Victor's elegance and Michael's magnetism. He nursed a drink, probably not his first, and it struck Hope suddenly that he had more to gain or lose from the outcome of the evening than anyone else. He had already lost two sons and now, by unforeseen circumstances, one of them may have returned to the fold. What kind of emotional upheaval had Michael's arrival in their lives caused Edward? And what effect would it have on him if Michael were to just as suddenly vanish?

For the first time in a long time, Hope felt a rush of sympathy for her father-in-law. His drinking had always disgusted her, but now she saw so clearly how the tragedy thirty-one years ago might have made him turn to the solace of the bottle. His three-year-old son had been kidnapped from his own home, and as a result, public sympathy for the Kingsley family had been so great that Edward had been elected governor several months later in a landslide victory. The guilt from capitalizing, even inadvertently, on his son's tragic disappearance must have been devastating.

"Hope," Iris said, spotting her just inside the doorway. "Now, we're all finally here." Her dark blue eyes raked the room, acknowledging in her own way everyone present. Her gaze warmed when it rested on Hope, beamed when she turned to Michael, softened fondly as she patted Victor's arm, saddened when she looked at Edward, and then, very subtly, hardened when it fell on Pamela, dressed in pristine white, and Jeremy, who leaned an elbow against the fireplace and stared at Michael.

From their expressions, Hope couldn't tell who knew what. It was maddening. Why couldn't Victor just tell them what *he* knew? Why put them through all this?

Because Iris wants her night, Hope thought. *And Iris always gets what she wants.*

As if reading her thoughts, Iris said, "Come sit by me, Hope." She patted the sofa next to her.

Hope, very much aware of Pamela and Jeremy watching her, moved across the room and sat down. Iris smiled in approval. "You look lovely tonight. Doesn't she, Michael?"

"Incredible," he agreed, his dark eyes mocking Hope.

Without warning, Iris lifted her hands and unfastened the heavy necklace from around her neck. Hope watched the sliding sparkle of diamonds and amethysts as Iris captured them in her hand. "There," she said, holding the necklace in her palm. "These would be wonderful with your dress."

Hope's hand flew to her throat. "Oh, I couldn't. They looked so beautiful on you."

"Nonsense. I'm an old woman. I have lots of necklaces. I want you to have this."

For some reason, it seemed important to Iris that Hope accept the necklace, and it was just as important to Hope that she did not. She shook her head. "You told me once this necklace was a gift. I couldn't possibly take it."

Iris sighed. "Very well, then. At least wear it tonight. You can return it to me in the morning."

It seemed a harmless enough request, but one Hope was still reluctant to grant. The necklace was yet another tie to the Kingsleys. However, Hope had little choice in the matter now. Iris was already reaching to fasten it around her neck, but then she stopped and said, "Michael, would you, please? My eyes aren't what they once were."

Michael took the necklace from Iris and stood. He gazed down at Hope expectantly, and she rose also, standing with her back to him. He draped the sparkling jewels around her neck, his fingers caressing her nape as he struggled with the clasp. A chill shot through Hope. She glanced up to find Jeremy's eyes not on her, but on the necklace. Then his gaze lifted, and she saw in those pale depths an emotion that looked very much like hatred.

Michael's finger slid along the bare skin of her neck. "There," he murmured. "Now, you're perfect."

"This night is perfect," Iris declared, watching Hope and Michael approvingly. "One I've dreamed about for a long, long time. Three generations of Kingsleys, all together again at long last."

"Careful," Michael warned, reclaiming his seat beside her. "Victor hasn't told you what the DNA results are yet."

Iris lifted her hand to Michael's cheek. "He doesn't have to. I know who you are. I've known all along." She turned, encompassing the whole group with her smile, but her gaze zeroed in on Hope. "There's only one thing that could make me happier at this moment. If there were a fourth generation to carry on the Kingsley name and tradition."

Hope's heart plummeted. Surely Iris wasn't still entertaining thoughts of her and Michael producing a Kingsley heir together. Hadn't he told Iris what she'd said? That as soon as everything was settled she was leaving?

Victor came up beside Hope. "Will you excuse us? I need to speak with Iris for a moment."

"Of course." Hope moved away as Victor sat down beside Iris and started talking to her in a low tone. Michael got up, also, and went over to engage Edward in conversation, while Pamela and Jeremy watched, as usual, from a distance.

Hope walked to the French doors and stared out. Something moved in the garden, and her heart leaped in alarm. Then she recognized the shadow. Glancing over her shoulder, assuring herself that everyone was preoccupied for the time being, she opened the door and slipped out into the softly falling twilight.

At the edge of the terrace, out of sight of anyone inside, she called softly, "Jake?"

"Over here."

She moved toward his voice, finding him in the deeper shadows of the garden. He wore jeans and a T-shirt, and his hair was damp, as if he'd just come from the shower.

For the longest moment, he stared down at her. "God, you're beautiful."

Hope touched the necklace with her fingertips, feeling the thud of her pulse against her throat. Strange after all this time that Jake could still do that to her.

"I used to see you this way sometimes when I'd be here visiting Pop. I'd watch you come out of the house, wearing something that cost more than I made in a month, and I'd think how perfect you looked. How much you belonged in a place like this."

"But you were wrong," Hope said softly. "This isn't me. The gown, the jewels, all the trappings of wealth. I tried to pretend I belonged here. At first, I even managed to convince myself this is what I wanted. But deep down, I knew I could never really fit in here. That I didn't even want to." She reached down and took his hand, drawing their linked fingers up to her cheek. "I'm a cop's daughter, Jake. I should have been a cop's wife."

His eyes closed briefly. "Do you know how long I've waited to hear you say that?"

"Too long," she whispered.

He loosened his fingers from hers and drew his knuckles down her cheek. "When all this is over..."

Her throat knotted. "I know."

He said nothing else, just stared down at her with a look that captured her breath. Words were not needed, but the emotion flowing between them was almost a tangible thing.

"I'd better get back inside," Hope said with a sigh. "Someone may come looking for me. I'll be in touch later to let you know what happens."

"You do that," he said, his gaze dark and intense. "Because I'll be waiting."

DINNER WAS A CAREFULLY orchestrated affair, but Hope couldn't quite figure out Iris's strategy behind the seating arrangement, although she knew there must have been one. Iris was at the head of the table, with Edward on her left and Michael on her right. But instead of placing Hope on Michael's right, as she'd expected and feared, she found herself seated between Edward and Victor Northrup.

Across the table, Pamela was to Michael's right, with Jeremy on her right, and every time Hope looked up, she found Jeremy's pale gaze upon her. What was he thinking? she wondered. Did he already know, as Jake suspected he did, who Michael Eldridge really was? Were Jeremy and Pamela responsible for bringing him here?

The courses were served and removed as the meal wore on, and Hope hardly remembered the taste of anything. She knew the food was delicious, though, because Iris wouldn't have it any other way. The sauces would be rich and creamy, the soup aromatic and savory, the lamb succulent and tender, the asparagus and rosemary potatoes fresh and seasoned to perfection. And the bottles of wine would have been carefully chosen from Iris's own private cellar to complement each course.

"You aren't eating much tonight," Victor commented, when yet another of Hope's plates had been removed virtually untouched.

She shrugged. "I had a late lunch."

Victor lifted his wineglass and examined the contents. "I was afraid you might have been offended by Iris's not-so-subtle comment about propagating the Kingsley line."

Hope blushed. "Iris has always wanted a great-grandchild. She's never made any bones about that."

"Yet you and Andrew never complied. I've always wondered why."

Hope shrugged, having no intention of getting into her and Andrew's private affairs with Victor, no matter how close he might be to the family.

"Iris is very fond of you, you know. She thinks of you as a granddaughter. I'm sure she'd like nothing more than to keep you in the family."

Hope glanced up at him. Had Iris said something to him about her wishes for Hope and Michael?

"I'm very fond of Iris as well," Hope said. "But I intend to move out of this house as soon as possible. My husband is dead. It's time I get on with my life."

"You could do that here," he replied. "Andrew's estate left you very little, but if you continue on at the mansion, you wouldn't have to worry about your future. Iris would make sure you never wanted for anything. And all you'd have to do…" He trailed off, gazing at her curiously. "Well. It's a little premature to be thinking long-term, isn't it? I haven't announced the DNA results yet."

The back of Hope's neck prickled with unease. He

may not have made the announcement yet, but she thought he'd just given her a significant clue as to how the tests had turned out.

THEY RETURNED TO THE library after dinner for coffee and for the Big News. Hope glanced around the room, trying to ascertain whether anyone other than Victor knew for certain what the outcome was, but no one gave himself or herself away. The identity of Michael's conspirators—if he had them—remained a mystery.

Finally, Iris set aside her cup and nodded to Victor who rose and took center stage near the fireplace. He removed an envelope from the inside pocket of his jacket and unfolded the contents.

"I'll spare you Dr. Wu's technical jargon," he said, "and get right to the point. According to the extensive tests performed on the blood samples provided by Michael and posthumously by Andrew, Dr. Wu has concluded that the DNA is as close a match as is humanly possible to determine. The only way that these two blood specimens could not belong to identical twins is if the same donor provided both samples. And we know that didn't happen. The blood was collected and sent from three separate locations—Michael's from Dr. Tremayne at his clinic, Andrew's from his private physician at Mercy General Hospital and from the Shepherd police. Therefore, it is Dr. Wu's conclusion that Michael Eldridge is Adam Kingsley."

There were no gasps or sputters of amazement. No one looked shocked, or even mildly surprised, and this in itself was astonishing to Hope. Not Iris's reaction, of course. She'd made it clear from the first that she had no doubt about Michael's identity.

But neither Jeremy or Pamela showed the slightest bit of surprise or even concern about the announcement, and Hope had to wonder again if they were the ones who had found Michael—Adam, she corrected herself—and brought him here. And to what end?

But if Jeremy and Pamela's reaction was troubling, Edward's response to the announcement was deeply moving. He sat quietly for a moment, as if it took him a bit longer than the others to take it all in, and then, setting his drink aside, he covered his face with his hands and wept.

Hope's heart went out to him. She stood near his chair and wondered if she should go to him, try to comfort him. But Michael beat her to it. He rose swiftly and crossed the distance to Edward, kneeling beside him.

"It's okay," he said, as if soothing a child. "I'm home now. Everything will be all right."

He lay his hand on Edward's shoulder, but he was looking up at Hope. And he was smiling.

Chapter Thirteen

It was nearly midnight before Hope was able to slip out of the house and make her way through the gardens to Jake's father's cottage. She still wore the lavender dress, but she'd removed Iris's necklace and locked it in her jewel box before she left. Now she wished she'd thought to throw on a sweater. The night chill had fallen as heavily as the darkness.

She paused outside the door to the cottage, hesitant to knock for fear she would disturb Jake's father. Finally, however, she rapped her knuckles as softly as she could against the wood, hoping that Jake would still be up and waiting for her.

The door opened almost instantly and he drew her inside. The warm coziness of the cottage wrapped around Hope like a downy blanket. She shivered, not from the cold, but from the way Jake looked at her.

"Is your father sleeping?" she asked quietly.

"He's not here. He drove down to Oxford this afternoon to be with his sister. She's having knee surgery tomorrow. He's going to stay down there and take care of her for a few days."

Hope glanced around the tiny living room, as if to dispute Jake's words. "So...we're alone?"

"Completely." He reached out and drew his hand down the bare skin of her arm. Hope shivered again. "Don't you want to know what happened tonight?"

"Dying to." But his eyes told her he wanted to hear something else.

"The DNA tests proved that Michael is Adam. He really is a Kingsley."

"Well," Jake said, "we thought that might be the case."

"I guess everyone else did, too. No one seemed surprised by the news."

"Maybe because at least some of them already knew." He paused for a moment, then tugged her ever so slightly toward him. "You know what that means, don't you?"

"What?"

"Andrew is really dead, Hope."

She drew a long breath. "I know."

"You aren't married anymore."

"I know that, too."

"We're both free." He cupped her face with his hands, gazing deeply into her eyes. "And now I think it's time I kiss you."

She smiled, her heart hammering inside her. "You've already done that."

"I mean, *really* kiss you."

"Oh…"

There was no time to say anything more because he bent swiftly and captured her lips with his, and Hope knew instantly what he meant. The other kisses they'd shared had only been preludes to this.

She closed her eyes, yielding to the temptation, letting the sensations sweep her away on a tide of romance and passion and the promise of what was to come.

Jake's lips possessed hers. His tongue invaded her mouth, conquering her resistance. And then, as the heat built inside her, she conquered him, kissing him, touching him, whispering to him words she'd never thought to say aloud.

They somehow made it to his bedroom—the same room he'd had as a boy, with the window that looked out on the Kingsley mansion. A pang of sadness whispered over Hope as she thought about Jake gazing out that window, seeing her from a distance, thinking she belonged in a house where he would never be welcome.

He saw her tears in the moonlight and raised himself on one elbow to stare down at her. "What's wrong?"

"When I think about what we had...all those wasted years..."

He wiped away her tears. "Don't look back, Hope. Not on those years. Think about what we had before, what we shared. It's still there. We didn't lose it, we just misplaced it for a while. The fact is, I love you. I've always loved you."

"Jake—"

He touched a fingertip to her lips, silencing her when she wanted so badly to tell him that she loved him, too; that she'd always loved him. But to admit that would seem like a betrayal of her marriage vows, something she still believed in and held sacred. Jake understood that. He knew her so well.

"I love you now," she said. "And I loved you then."

He bent to kiss her, softly at first. But then, as she

wrapped her arms around him and molded her body to his, the heat began to build all over again.

"And that's enough," he said. "That's everything."

A DREAM AWAKENED HOPE. A nightmare, really. The images had been powerful. She was at Andrew's funeral, but instead of a closed casket as it had been in reality, the lid of his coffin was open and she was gazing down at him, thinking how very peaceful he looked. And then suddenly, his eyes were staring into hers, and he grabbed her hand, pulling her toward the casket. "I won't let him have you," he warned in a voice as cold and deadly as the grave. "I'll see you both dead first."

And then a faceless voice with an Oriental accent said, "The only way these two blood specimens could not belong to identical twins is if the same donor provided both samples... Provided both samples... Provided both samples..."

Hope had awakened in a cold sweat, that same phrase echoing in her head, as a growing horror dawned inside her.

What if Andrew had provided both of those samples? What if the reason Michael Eldridge had never been worried about the DNA tests was because he *knew* what the results would be?

He knew...because he was Andrew.

Hope put her hands to her face. No, she thought. It couldn't be. It wasn't possible.

But it was the only thing that made sense. Michael Eldridge was *too* much like Andrew. There was no way even an identical twin, especially one who had been raised apart, could be that much like Andrew.

Michael Eldridge was Andrew. He was still Hope's husband. And she had just...

Her gaze flew to Jake's sleeping form. He lay on his back, one arm hanging over the side of the bed, the other flung over his head, and she thought again how much she loved him, how much she needed him. What she had to do to protect him.

"I'll see you both dead first."

She had to get out of here before Andrew saw them. Before his rage consumed him.

As quietly as she could, Hope got up and slipped on the lavender gown, carrying the high-heeled sandals with her until she'd let herself out the front door. Then, after tugging on her shoes, she made her way through the gardens.

The night, so beautiful a short while ago, now grew heavy with Hope's dread. What should she do? How could she find out the truth? How could she expose Andrew's lies and deception without threatening Jake's life?

She skirted the pool, trying to keep to the shadows, but just as he had the other night, Michael rose from one of the lounge chairs to startle her. She still couldn't bring herself to call him Andrew, even in her mind. Somehow, if she still thought of him as Michael, he couldn't hurt her. He couldn't hurt Jake.

He came toward her in the darkness, and Hope knew immediately something was different. She started to turn and run, but he lunged forward and caught her, spinning her around to face him in the moonlight.

"Who would have thought," he said coldly, "that our little Hope, the very epitome of loyalty and sacrifice, would commit the ultimate sin against her marriage vows? You were with him tonight. Don't try to deny it.''

Hope's heart pounded in her ears. She tried to steady her nerves, but his eyes were so cold. As cold as the eyes in her dream. And just as deadly. "Why do you care?" she managed to ask him. "You're Adam."

From his pocket, he pulled out a gold chain, holding it up in the moonlight. A medallion, a one-sided coin, dangled from the chain, and Hope gasped as she recognized it. Iris had given the coins to Adam and Andrew on their third birthday. Andrew never took his off. He'd been wearing it the night he was supposedly killed.

"I never fooled you, did I, Hope? Everyone believed I was Adam, but not you. You knew. From the first, you knew we belonged together."

Hope tried to struggle from his grasp, but he held her tighter, hauling her against him until she could hardly breathe. He ran a hand through her hair. "I want what's mine," he said. "I want what I've been waiting for for years." He tried to kiss her, but Hope jerked her head away.

He laughed. "Maybe you won't have quite so much fight in you once your lover is dead."

Fear froze in her veins. She had to get away, warn Jake he was in danger. Michael...Andrew was a madman. Something had come unhinged inside him.

But even as she struggled to free herself, she saw another man coming toward them in the garden. At first she thought it was Jake and tried to cry out a warning, but Michael's hand clamped over her mouth. Her fear deepened as the other man moved from the shadows into the moonlight, and she recognized him.

"Let's get this over with," he said. "Hurry up."

Michael dropped his hand from her mouth long enough to pull a saturated cloth from his pocket. In the brief instant it took him to raise it to her face, Hope screamed. Then he slapped the cloth over her mouth and nose, stifling the noise, and panic bubbled up inside her. She couldn't breathe. Within seconds the fumes overpowered her. Her knees buckled and she slipped silently to the ground.

JAKE CAME AWAKE instantly at Hope's scream and bolted upright in bed. At first he thought he might have dreamed the sound, but the empty side of the bed where Hope had lain a short while ago spurred him into action. He jerked on his jeans and grabbed his gun, then crept through the house like a ghost.

Satisfied that the noise hadn't come from inside, Jake opened the front door and slipped out. He paused for a moment, listening to the darkness. When he would have stolen through the gardens toward the main house, a voice beside him said, "We've got her. If you want to see her alive, drop the gun."

Jake knew that voice. It was the same one he'd heard in the warehouse in Houston. He turned his head a fraction of an inch, and Jonas Thorpe came into view.

"Drop the gun," he advised again. "Remember, I've got that itchy trigger-finger Pratt warned you about."

This was the third time Thorpe had gotten the jump on him, and Jake swore inwardly. There would be a score to settle later, once Hope was safe. For now, though, he had little choice. His gun dropped to the ground.

"Now back inside," Thorpe ordered, aiming his own weapon at Jake's heart.

Jake slowly backed into the house. Once inside, Thorpe threw him a pair of handcuffs. "Appropriate for an ex-cop, don't you think? Around your right wrist and the arm of the chair." When Jake hesitated, Thorpe said, "You don't want to make things any more uncomfortable for that pretty little girlfriend of yours, now do you?"

Jake sat down in the chair, but he didn't fasten the handcuffs. "How do I know you have her?"

Thorpe fished in his pocket and produced the diamond clasp Hope had worn in her hair. "If you need more proof, I can bring you one of her fingers."

"Where is she? I want to see her." Even though his options were limited at the moment, Jake knew that if Hope had been harmed, he would find a way to make Thorpe pay. Thorpe could count on that.

"Put the handcuffs on and then we'll talk," Thorpe told him.

Jake slipped one of the cuffs over his wrist, then fastened the other to the arm of the chair.

Thorpe smiled. "That should slow you down if you decide to make a run for it."

"Where's Hope? If you've so much as touched her, I swear I'll kill you."

Thorpe propped his foot on a chair and folded his arms across his knee, keeping the gun pointed at Jake. "You're not exactly in any position to be making threats, now are you?"

Jake glared at him. "What do you want?"

"Unfortunately for you, you'll find that out soon enough."

The front door of the cottage opened, and Michael

Eldridge walked in. He still wore the tuxedo he'd had on earlier for dinner, but the tie was slightly askew and there were bits of leaves and grass on his pants.

"Everything all taken care of?" Thorpe asked.

Eldridge shrugged. "It soon will be. What about him?" He nodded toward Jake.

"I'm waiting to hear from the boss. Soon as I do, we move him."

"Why don't we take care of him now?" Eldridge's eyes glinted dangerously. He pulled a gun from his pocket and walked over to Jake, aiming the barrel at his temple. He cocked the trigger. "I ought to kill you right now. When I think of you touching her—"

"Cut the jealous-husband routine," Thorpe said impatiently. "You're supposed to be *Adam* Kingsley, you idiot."

Eldridge swung the gun toward Thorpe. "Don't call me that. Don't ever call me that."

"All right, *Einstein.*"

"Where's Hope?" Jake asked Eldridge. "What have you done to her?"

Eldridge grinned, and Jake thought the glimmer of madness in his eyes must have been what Clarence Donovan had glimpsed in Michael's picture. "Nothing yet. I'm taking her back to where it all began. An appropriate ending for an adulteress, don't you think?"

Jake surged toward Eldridge, but he had the advantage of not being bound to a chair. In a flash, he smashed the gun against Jake's temple and Jake's skull exploded with pain. He fell back against the chair, blood streaming down his face. His last conscious thought was that Hope had been right: Andrew had come back from the grave.

WHEN JAKE CAME TO, he found himself slumped in the seat of his Blazer, his right wrist handcuffed to the steering wheel. The window was down, and he could hear voices outside. He eased himself up, peering out into the darkness.

They appeared to be miles from the city. He could see the distant glow of lights, the silhouette of treetops against the sky, and below him, the glitter of moonlight on water.

His truck was parked on a high bluff overlooking the river. It didn't take much imagination to figure out what Thorpe had in store for him. One good nudge, and the Blazer would go over the cliff, plunging into the river with Jake trapped inside. They'd even thought to roll down the windows so the truck would sink faster.

The voices outside grew louder, as if they were arguing. Even as Jake's mind worked frantically for a way to free himself, he strained to hear what they were saying.

"...sure he knew where to bring her? You made everything clear?" asked a cultured-sounding voice. A voice that definitely did not belong to Simon Pratt, as Jake had been expecting. He eased himself up a little higher.

Three people stood near the edge of the bluff, off to the left of the truck. Even though their backs were to him, Jake recognized Thorpe and the slender silhouette of a woman. The other man stood apart from those two, facing them, and Jake saw moonlight glinting in silver hair. The regal bearing and the cultured voice were unmistakeable.

Victor Northrup was the "boss" Jake had heard Thorpe and Benny talking about in Houston. But why the hell was Thorpe working for him instead of Simon Pratt?

"He knew where to come," Thorpe said in response to Northrup's question. He paused for a moment. "But he was acting crazy. Crazier than usual. I think he may have gone off the deep end this time."

"Damn," said Northrup. "I was counting on Hope to keep him in line."

"You can forget that," Thorpe said. "He's convinced she's betrayed him. I really think the crazy bastard believes he's Andrew Kingsley."

"He's never been stable," Northrup agreed. "And it didn't help when, after years of training to become Andrew, he suddenly had to become Adam."

What the hell were they talking about? Training to become Andrew and then had to suddenly become Adam? Was Eldridge an impostor after all?

Jake tried to process this information while he dug in his pocket for something metal. Years ago, he'd busted a small-time hoodlum named Tony the Greek who had a talent for picking just about any lock ever designed. After the third time he'd picked the lock on his handcuffs and escaped, Jake had hauled him back in and made him demonstrate the procedure. After a few tries with a paper clip, Jake had managed to open the cuffs himself. For his sake and Hope's, he fervently hoped he still remembered how.

Jake's office and house keys had been removed from his pockets, and he knew he didn't have a prayer of finding a paper clip in his truck. But he always kept a pen in his console. Reaching across with his left hand, he pushed the button on the console and the lid flew up. The sound made him wince, and he quickly glanced outside, pausing for a moment to listen.

"If Michael said he'd be here, he'll be here," the woman was saying. "Let's give him a little more time."

"I say we get rid of McClain now, and then we do Hope as soon as Eldridge shows up with her."

"Aren't you two forgetting something?" Northrup asked coldly. "His name is Adam. You'd better start thinking of him that way from here on out. One mistake could be the end of us."

"You mean a mistake like McClain?" Thorpe asked.

If possible, Northrup's tone grew even icier. "He won't be a problem for much longer, and neither will Hope, more's the pity."

Jake located the pen and quickly unscrewed the top, dumping out the ink cartridge and spring into the palm of his left hand. He discarded everything but the metal spring, which he pulled taut, fashioning himself a miniature jimmy. Tony the Greek had taught him how to pick the lock while both hands were cuffed behind his back. With one hand free, even if it was his left, the maneuver should be a cinch, he told himself.

He set to work, keeping an eye on the three figures outside the truck window. After a few moments, Northrup turned back to Thorpe.

"Damn!" he snarled. "Where could he be? He's going to ruin everything."

"Maybe he isn't coming," Thorpe said. "He mentioned something about taking Hope back to the place where it all began."

"The place where it all began? What the hell did he mean by that?" Northrup demanded.

"I thought he was just yanking McClain's chain, but maybe he wasn't. Maybe I should go look for him."

"No." Northrup's voice was firm and decisive. "You stay here and take care of McClain. Carol and I will go find...Adam."

There was a momentary flurry of activity while Northrup and Carol climbed into his silver Rolls-Royce, and he issued last-minute instructions to Thorpe. Then the engine started up, the car lights came on, and Jake slid back down in the seat.

As the sound of the motor faded away, he expected to see Thorpe at the window at any moment. Jake continued to work at the lock, keeping his fingers as steady as possible while his heart pounded inside him. He knew he only had seconds....

The lock sprang open, and Jake pulled his hand free. He glanced out the window, trying to locate Thorpe. Another car engine roared to life, and Jake jerked around toward the sound. In the darkness, he could see a vehicle moving up behind his Blazer. Thorpe meant to ram him off the cliff.

Jake's fist shot up and shattered the interior light. He closed his hand over the door handle as he felt the jarring impact of the collision. In a moment, the front wheels of the Blazer would go over the cliff. Jake's timing had to be exact.

As the truck tilted sharply forward, Jake opened the door and tumbled out. There was a small patch of bushes near the edge of the cliff, and he rolled toward it for cover.

Behind him, he heard the sound of the Blazer going

over the bluff and then a brief moment of silence before he heard the hard splash below.

The smashed light hadn't come on in the Blazer when he'd opened the door, and he wasn't sure if Thorpe had seen him leap from the truck or not. Thorpe backed his own vehicle from the edge of the cliff and turned toward the road. The lights were still off, but he left the motor idling as he opened the door and climbed out.

The gun in Thorpe's hand gleamed in the moonlight as he slowly walked back toward the bluff. The small clump of bushes was Jake's only cover, so it wouldn't take long for Thorpe to find him. Jake crouched, ready to spring, as Thorpe neared the edge of the cliff and stood looking down at the water. And then he laughed—a deep, satisfied sound, which Jake took as his cue.

He lunged from the bushes and grabbed Thorpe's legs, jerking him downward with all his strength. He heard Thorpe's grunt of surprise just before he fell with a thud to the ground. His gun sprang free, and he scrambled toward it, but Jake grabbed him again. Thorpe kicked him in the face, and Jake fell back toward the edge of the cliff.

In a flash, Thorpe was on him, pressing his advantage, pushing Jake closer and closer to the edge. Jake managed to get his hands around Thorpe's neck, and as Thorpe tried to free himself, they both slid over the cliff, crashing into a jagged ledge five feet from the top.

Jake grabbed for a purchase, and his fingers closed around a sharp, jutting rock. He clung to the rock, looking around wildly in the darkness for Thorpe. He had also found a handhold, but it looked more precarious than Jake's. As Jake watched, the bit of rock Thorpe hung from crumbled away from the ledge, and he fell into the river thirty feet below.

Jake didn't think the fall would have killed Thorpe, but he didn't have time to find out. He pulled himself back up to the ledge, then climbed to the top of the bluff. Picking up Thorpe's gun from the ground, he ran toward Thorpe's truck.

A cell phone lay in the passenger seat, and as Jake tore down the dirt road toward the city lights, he dialed Brant Colter's home number.

"I need you to put out an APB on a silver Rolls-Royce registered to Victor Northrup."

There was a pause, then Brant's sleep-slurred voice said, "Who the hell is this?"

"It's Jake. Jake McClain. I don't have time to explain, but I need you to have Northrup and his blond companion picked up and brought in for questioning. They may be armed and dangerous."

"What are we supposed to question them about?" Brant demanded.

"The murder of Andrew Kingsley, for starters." Jake cut off Brant's explosive string of questions and said, "I don't have time to explain it all now. I need you to issue another APB on a red Dodge Viper with Texas plates, registered to a Michael Eldridge. He may be armed and dangerous, too, and he's got Hope."

He hung up the phone and tossed it back to the seat. Ahead of him, the lights of the Memphis-Arkansas bridge arced across the river, and beyond, the glow of Riverside Drive and downtown Memphis. As he raced across the bridge, something in the skyline caught his eye. The lighted spires of Saint Mary's Cathedral, where Hope and Andrew had been married.

The place where it had all begun.

Chapter Fourteen

Hope opened her eyes on a wave of nausea and fear. She lay still, trying to quiet her rolling stomach. After a few moments, she sat up and glanced around. Terror washed over as she slowly took in her surroundings.

She was in the candlelit bell tower of a church. A three-foot wooden wall enclosed the tower, while an opening in the floor near where she sat led down to a steep set of stairs.

The bell loomed over her, gleaming in the candlelight. As she struggled to her feet, a voice from the other side of the enclosure said, "You've been out for a long time. I'd begun to wonder if you were ever coming to."

He came out of the shadows then and walked slowly toward her. Reflected candlelight flickered in his eyes, giving them a strange, glowing quality that frightened Hope even more.

"Where are we?" she asked, trying to suppress her terror. If this man was really Andrew, surely she could reason with him. He'd once loved her, hadn't he?

He stopped before her, smiling down at her. "You know where we are, Hope. I told you I was taking you to the place where it all began for us. Don't you remember?''

Saint Mary's, she thought. She pictured the structure in her mind, the magnificent stained-glass windows, the lighted spires, and the bell tower a good fifty feet above the ground. How had he gotten her up here? And what did he plan to do with her?

As if he'd read her mind, his smile deepened. ''I thought we might renew our vows, Hope. I want to hear you say that you'll love, honor and cherish me until death do us part.''

All hope of reasoning with him fled. She could see the madness in his eyes. ''Don't do this,'' she begged.

He grabbed her arms and hauled her toward him. ''Say it, damn you! Say it! Until death do us part!'' He walked her backward, until she was bent over the wall that overlooked the street far below. ''Say it!''

Hope grabbed for the wall. She could feel her feet lifting from the floor. Another few inches and she would fall backward over the wall, to the ground far below. Jake would be next. She wouldn't be able to warn him, and Andrew would have his revenge.

''I'll say it,'' she said, glancing downward. Her head swam dizzily. She squeezed her eyes closed. ''Let me up and I'll say whatever you want me to.''

He hesitated, then pulled her up to face him. His smile grew triumphant. ''Till death do us part, Hope.''

She opened her mouth to say the words, but before she could utter a sound, another voice spoke from the trap door. ''You forgot to ask if anyone objects to this union,'' Jake said.

He emerged from the opening and stood facing them. Hope's heart pounded in terror, not just for herself, but for Jake. Andrew would kill him. She had no doubt about that.

Andrew grabbed Hope and jerked her up against him. "You shouldn't have come here, Jake. You don't belong here."

Jake walked slowly toward them. "Let her go. This is between you and me."

Andrew's arm tightened around Hope's throat. "Where's your gun? I know you didn't come here empty-handed." When Jake didn't respond, he shoved Hope toward the wall again. "Get rid of the gun, Jake, or she and I both go over the wall."

Jake's gaze flashed to Hope, then back to Andrew. He reached around and drew his gun from the back of his belt, then knelt and slid it across the floor. Andrew kicked the weapon aside, and drew his own gun, leveling it at Jake.

"You're a fool, McClain. Pining after her all these years when all along, she was meant for me."

As he spoke, his arm loosened around Hope's throat. She saw his finger tighten on the trigger, and instinctively, she shoved her elbow into his stomach as hard as she could. The gun went off, and she saw Jake fall to the floor.

Since Andrew was caught by surprise, his arm slipped from Hope's throat. She jerked away from him and lunged for the gun on the floor just as Jake came crashing into Andrew. The momentum flung them against the wooden wall, and in horror, Hope heard the crack of a board as it gave way.

Her breath in her throat, she watched helplessly as the two men struggled for a moment, and then Jake lost his footing and plunged through the opening in the wall.

Hope screamed, leaping forward to try and save him. To her relief, she saw that he'd managed to cling to the wooden floorboards, but he was dangling in midair fifty feet above the ground.

She started toward him, but Andrew whirled, the gun still in his hand. Hope had a weapon, too, and she leveled it at him. The two of them faced off, and then Andrew grinned. "You can't kill me, Hope. You and I are meant to be together."

"Move back," she said. "Get away from him."

Slowly, very deliberately, Andrew turned and pointed his gun downward at Jake.

Without hesitating, Hope squeezed the trigger on Jake's gun, and the report inside the bell tower almost deafened her. Andrew gazed down at the red bloom on his shirt, then back up at her. He looked puzzled, as if he couldn't quite figure out what had gone wrong. Then, almost in slow motion, he crashed through the splintered wood and fell with a horrified scream to the street below.

Hope went to help Jake, but he'd already hitched himself up to the floor of the bell tower. They sat quietly for a moment, Jake breathing deeply from the exertion and Hope in shock. She began to tremble all over.

"I killed him," she finally said, rubbing the back of her hand across the moisture on her face. "I killed Andrew."

"Hope, listen to me." Jake took her by the shoulders and turned her to face him. "He wasn't Andrew. Andrew died in that car crash. He was murdered."

She glanced up at him. "Then who—?"

"I don't know all the details," Jake said. "I'm hoping once the police pick up Victor Northrup, we'll have our answers, but for right now—'' he brushed the hair from her face and gazed down at her ''—I just want to hold you.''

''I want that, too,'' she whispered. ''More than you'll ever know.''

BRANT COLTER STEPPED out of the interrogation room and walked over to where Jake and Hope sat waiting.

''You're not going to believe this,'' he said.

Jake removed his arm from Hope's shoulder and stood. ''After tonight, I'll believe anything.''

''Northrup's willing to talk. He's ready to finger the Grayson Commission in return for a deal.''

Jake's jaw tightened. ''There's no way he can walk.''

''Hell, no,'' Brant agreed. ''The D.A. might consider a reduced sentence, though, depending on what he gives us. But you know what the real kicker is? He wants to talk to you. In fact, he won't talk to anyone else.''

''You're kidding. What do the brass have to say about that?''

Brant grinned. ''They're pissed, but Northrup's adamant. It's you or no one. I'd say this is a little payback, wouldn't you?''

Jake shrugged. He no longer cared about getting back at the department. He just wanted the truth. And he wanted Hope.

He glanced down at her. She'd had a rough night, and it was likely to get worse. Once they finished here, they would have to go tell Iris.

''I'll be back as soon as I can,'' he told her. ''You want me to get someone to take you home?''

She shook her head. ''No way. I'll wait for you.''

He nodded. Their gazes clung for a moment, and then he turned and followed Brant down the hallway to the interrogation room.

NORTHRUP LOOKED UP as Jake entered. Impatience flickered across his arrogant features. "None of this would have been necessary if you'd taken the case from me, you know."

"So it's all my fault," Jake said, sitting down across the table from him.

Northrup shrugged. "In a manner of speaking, yes. I would have steered you in the direction I wanted you to go, alleviating any suspicion from me in the process, but Hope came along, and you had to do her bidding, didn't you? A pity for all of us."

"Why don't you start at the beginning?" Jake suggested. "Who was Michael Eldridge?"

Not even a flicker of emotion crossed Northrup's features at Jake's use of the past tense. He smoothed back his hair with the palm of his hand, as if grooming himself for an important meeting. "He was exactly who he claimed to be—a stockbroker from Houston leading a life that was carefully orchestrated for him from the time he was fifteen years old, when I first met him." Northrup paused, glancing at Jake. "You found out about his police record, and from that you've probably deduced I learned about him through his lawyer. I was in Houston twenty years ago trying to convince a young attorney named Charles McGee to join our firm here in Memphis when our meeting was interrupted by one of his clients, a juvenile delinquent named Michael Eldridge. When he burst into McGee's office, I very nearly had a heart attack. Even then, he looked a great deal like Andrew, but of course, years of training and a dozen plastic surgeries have refined his appearance. Not to mention his manners."

"How did you manage to convince a fifteen-year-old delinquent to join an underground political movement?" Jake asked.

Northrup smiled. "It wasn't hard to convince Michael to help us out once he understood the stakes involved. And, of course, the rewards. The difficult part was keeping him on the straight and narrow all these years. He has...had a tendency to be impulsive, shall we say, and except for that one unfortunate incident that brought him into our organization, we couldn't afford to have even a breath of scandal attached to his name. His background had to check out, his slate had to be clean in order for our plan to work."

"Which was getting him elected to office, right?"

"Exactly. Eventually the highest office in the land. The Grayson Commission has been very successful on state and local levels, but less so nationally. Michael—or rather, Adam Kingsley—was going to change all that."

"There's one thing I haven't been able to figure out," Jake said.

Northrup's arrogant smile flashed again. "Just one?"

"No one knew Adam Kingsley was still alive until last year, when DNA tests were performed on the remains in his grave. But you're telling me this plan has been in the works for years. How were you going to pull that off? How were you going to arrange for Adam to return from the dead?"

Northrup traced a set of carved initials in the

wooden table with his fingertips. "It can't have escaped your notice how very much like *Andrew* our Michael was. Not just his looks, but his actions, his speech patterns, even his walk."

"You're saying he was originally meant to take Andrew's place?"

"He studied tapes and recordings of Andrew for years, learning every nuance of Andrew's appearance, speech and mannerisms. When Andrew married Hope, we knew our greatest challenge would lie in convincing her. However, if we'd continued on with our original plan, that problem wouldn't have been as difficult to overcome as we'd thought. You see, in studying videos and photographs of Hope and Andrew together, Michael became very...enamored of her. He wanted her for himself, and so he rose to the challenge, as it were. Eventually, he became so adept at playing the role of Andrew that he sometimes forgot who he really was."

"Finding out the real Adam Kingsley was still alive must have thrown a monkey wrench into your plans," Jake said with grim amusement.

"You have no idea," Northrup said. "We couldn't take the chance that another Kingsley heir might someday turn up and want his share of the pie. So we changed our plans."

"And Michael became Adam instead of Andrew. But Andrew still had to go, didn't he?"

Northrup glanced up. "We could afford only one Kingsley heir. Divided power is no power at all."

"So how did you pull off the DNA tests?" Jake asked. "Were all three of the samples from Andrew?"

"Tell me something, Jake." Northrup sat back in

his chair and eyed Jake coolly. "If you were in my position, how would you make certain the DNA tests yielded the results you wanted, namely, that Michael was Adam Kingsley?"

Jake shrugged. "I'd have to find a way to switch his blood sample with a sample of Andrew's blood. Identical twins' DNA would be a match."

"Yes, but Andrew's been dead for five months. Wouldn't a forensics expert of Dr. Wu's caliber be able to tell that the sample hadn't been taken recently?"

Jake shrugged again. "You tell me."

"The one sure way to get the results we wanted was to switch Michael's blood with that of the real Adam Kingsley."

Jake stared at Northrup's smug countenance for a long, silent moment, digesting what he'd just told him. "Are you saying you know the whereabouts of the *real* Adam Kingsley? That you managed to somehow get him to cooperate with this...plan of yours?"

Northrup laughed softly. "You give me a little too much credit, I'm afraid. As it happens, I don't know Adam Kingsley's whereabouts. But Jonas Thorpe does."

And Thorpe had yet to be found. "How did you and Thorpe hook up?"

"Jonas came to me after the Adam Kingsley story broke last year, because he'd learned our firm handled all claims against the Kingsley estate. He wanted to know how much money Iris Kingsley would be willing to pay to learn the whereabouts of her long-lost grandson, but I persuaded Jonas to join us instead. He knew nothing about the Grayson Commission or Michael Eldridge at that point, but when I explained, he quickly understood how much more profitable our plan would be in the long run than a one-time payoff from Iris.''

''That still doesn't tell me how Thorpe knew about Adam.''

''As it turned out, Jonas's sister was the woman who helped kidnapped Adam all those years ago. She raised him as her own son. To this day, he hasn't a clue to his real identity. Can you imagine that?''

When Jake didn't comment, Northrup continued. ''Jonas didn't know who the boy was either until the story about Adam still being alive made headlines all over the country last year. Then, fortunately for us, he started to remember things from his sister's past—like how she'd disappeared from Memphis without a trace all those years ago, and how years later, when he finally saw her again, she had a son but no husband. A son who looked nothing like her or anyone else in the family. And she seemed extremely nervous, anxious to be rid of Jonas. So after the story about Adam broke, Jonas located his sister again, forced her to admit the truth to him, and then later, after he'd spoken with me, he convinced her to help us get a blood sample from Adam—unbeknownst to Adam, of course. Carol, substituting for the receptionist at the clinic, switched Adam's blood with Michael's. It was a brilliant scheme,'' he said, his eyes gleaming with pride. ''You have to admit that.''

Jake stood. ''You get points for long-term planning. And where you're going, you'll have plenty of time to come up with another one.''

Northrup smiled up at him. ''You don't really think I'll go to prison, do you? I have the best attorneys in the state at my beck and call. I won't spend a night behind bars.''

"We'll see about that." Jake headed for the door.

"Jake?"

He turned. Northrup was studying his fingernails. "Give my regards to Hope."

In your dreams, Jake thought and closed the door between them.

AT FIRST, IRIS HADN'T wanted to believe them, but when Hope and Jake finally convinced her, her blue eyes hardened with icy rage. "All these years, he pretended to be my friend, my confidant, while all along planning to destroy my family. He will never again see the light of day," she vowed. "I promise you that. Andrew's death will be avenged."

They had also told her about Michael Eldridge and his ultimate demise, and though Hope knew Iris had to be grieving for the grandson she'd hoped to reclaim, she held herself together remarkably well, probably because of her fury. When that subsided, the shock would set in. To be on the safe side, Hope had put in a call to her doctor.

"Do you think what he said about Adam is true?" Iris asked Jake. Her eyes misted, but she visibly fought the emotion. "The real Adam, I mean."

"I don't know," Jake said. "Unless and until we find Jonas Thorpe, we have only Northrup's word."

"But the woman who took Adam. Thorpe's sister. Surely she wouldn't be that hard to locate."

Jake met Iris's gaze evenly. "It's been over thirty years since she left Memphis. I'm sure she's changed her identity, probably several times since then, and there's no telling where she is now. Without Thorpe's help, it could be a little like looking for a needle in a haystack.''

"Then you'd better get started, hadn't you?" Iris's chin lifted and she glared at Jake.

He glared back. "Are you saying you want to hire me to find your grandson, Mrs. Kingsley?"

"That's exactly what I'm saying."

Jake shrugged. "I don't come cheap."

"I didn't expect you would." She turned to Hope. "I suppose you'll be leaving me now."

Hope started to deny it, but then she realized Iris no longer needed her. She had something other than her grief to focus on. She had a mission.

"It's time for me to move on," Hope said softly, and realized that no truer words had ever been spoken.

Hope took Jake's hand, and they left the Kingsley mansion together. As they drove east, into the beginning of a beautiful sunrise, Hope never once looked back.

A FEW HOURS LATER, Jake picked her up from her mother's house where he had taken her earlier. Hope had had a shower, changed clothes, and even managed to sleep for a little while. She woke up feeling refreshed, as if the weight of the world had been removed from her shoulders.

Joanna, her eyes glistening with emotion, hugged them both before they left. Hope felt near tears herself. After all these years, after all they'd been through, she and Jake had finally managed to find their way back to each other.

"Where are we going?" she asked, when Jake had backed out of her mother's driveway.

"You'll see."

Something in his voice made her curious. Hope turned to study his profile, but his expression gave nothing away.

Rather than leaving the neighborhood, he drove two blocks over, to Mrs. Forsythe's house. The For Sale sign had been removed from the front yard, and Hope glanced at him in surprise.

"What are we doing here, Jake?"

He parked the truck and turned off the ignition. Dangling a set of keys in front of her, he said, "Let's go in."

"How did you get those keys?"

"I happen to know the real-estate agent," he said. "She's the same lady who sold my house for me."

Jake let them into the house, and Hope looked around. All the furniture had been removed, but she could tell the place had been lovingly cared for. The hardwood floors gleamed, the windows sparkled, and the pastel walls glowed softly in the afternoon sunlight. She loved it immediately, just as she'd known she would the day she'd driven by here.

She turned to Jake, her tone suspicious. "How did you know about this house?"

"How do you think?"

"Let me take a wild guess. My mother the matchmaker, right?"

He grinned. "Let's look around."

He showed her the living room, the dining room, and the kitchen with a small, enclosed sunporch attached. When he started down the hall toward the bedrooms, Hope caught his arm.

"Jake, whose house is this?"

His eyes glowed with an inner light. He bent down and kissed her. "It could be ours."

She caught her breath. "Are you asking me to marry you?" She saw something flash in his eyes, a vulnerability she'd never seen there. Before he could respond, she said, "Because if you are, the answer is yes."

"Just like that?"

"Just like that. Ten years is a long time to wait. I wouldn't have blamed you if you'd married someone else. You had every right."

"There was never anyone but you," he said. "There never could be."

He took her hand and led her into the bedroom. Sunlight spilled through the many windows, highlighting the sleeping bag Jake had fashioned into a makeshift bed. Some of the windows were open and a breeze drifted through. A crystal vase of spring flowers—from her mother's garden, Hope would have sworn—was placed near the sleeping bag.

Jake sat and pulled her down beside him.

"I can't give you a ring," he said regretfully. "At least, not yet. It'll take the last of my savings to make a down payment on this house."

"I don't have any money, either," Hope said, but at the moment, she'd never felt so rich. Or so happy. She reached up and took his face between her hands. "I do love you, Jake. More than I ever thought possible."

He kissed her, and Hope wound her arms around his neck. They tumbled backward onto the sleeping bag, desire building deliciously. The breeze stirred the sweet, delicate scent of the flowers, reminding Hope of the first time they'd been together.

As if reading her mind, Jake whispered, "You're so perfect. Everywhere I touch. Here." He kissed her neck. "Here." His hand cupped her breast. "Here." His fingers skimmed down her stomach. "And here..."

"You remember," she breathed.

"Until the day I die," he said.

HARLEQUIN®

I N T R I G U E®

When little Adam Kingsley was taken from his nursery in the Kingsley mansion, the Memphis family used all their power and prestige to punish the kidnapper. They believed the crime was solved and the villain condemned...though the boy was never returned. But now, new evidence comes to light that may reveal the truth about...

The Kingsley Baby

Amanda Stevens is at her best for this powerful trilogy of a sensational crime and the three couples whose love lights the way to the truth. Don't miss:

#453 THE HERO'S SON (February)

#458 THE BROTHER'S WIFE (March)

#462 THE LONG-LOST HEIR (April)

What *really* happened that night in the Kingsley nursery?

**Look for these titles—
available at your favorite retail outlet!**

January 1998
Renegade Son by Lisa Jackson

Danielle Summers had problems: a rebellious child
and unscrupulous enemies. In addition, her Montana
ranch was slowly being sabotaged. And then there was
Chase McEnroe—who admired her land and desired her
body. But Danielle feared he would invade more than just
her property—he'd trespass on her heart.

February 1998
The Heart's Yearning by Ginna Gray

Fourteen years ago Laura gave her baby up for adoption,
and not one day had passed that she didn't think about
him and agonize over her choice—so she finally followed
her heart to Texas to see her child. But the plan to watch
her son from afar doesn't quite happen that way, once the
boy's sexy—*single*—father takes a decided interest in *her*.

March 1998
First Things Last by Dixie Browning

One look into Chandler Harrington's dark eyes and
Belinda Massey could refuse the Virginia millionaire nothing.
So how could the no-nonsense nanny believe the rumors that
he had kidnapped his nephew—an adorable, healthy little boy
who crawled as easily into her heart as he did into her lap?

**BORN IN THE USA: Love, marriage—
and the pursuit of family!**

Look us up on-line at: http://www.romance.net

BUSA4

Available in March 1998
from bestselling author

CATHERINE LANIGAN

Her genius would change the world...

When Karen creates Mastermind, the beautiful computer whiz isn't completely prepared to deal with people's reaction to it. On the one hand, two men have fallen in love with her. On the other, someone wants the program badly enough to threaten her roommate and attack her. Karen doesn't know who to trust—and for all its power, that's the one question her computer isn't programmed to answer....

TENDER MALICE

"Catherine Lanigan is a master storyteller."
—*Rave Reviews*

Coming to your favorite retail outlet.

This April
DEBBIE MACOMBER

takes readers to the Big Sky and beyond...

MONTANA

At her grandfather's request, Molly packs up her kids and returns to his ranch in Sweetgrass, Montana.

But when she arrives, she finds a stranger, Sam Dakota, working there. Molly has questions: What exactly is he doing there? Why doesn't the sheriff trust him? Just *who* is Sam Dakota? These questions become all the more critical when her grandfather tries to push them into marriage....

Moving to the state of Montana is one thing; entering the state of matrimony is quite another!

Available in April 1998 wherever books are sold.

She's a woman without a future
because of her past.

THE
DAUGHTER

At fifteen, Maggie is convicted of her mother's
murder. Seven years later she escapes from
prison to prove her innocence.

After many years on the run, Maggie makes a
dangerous decision: to trust Sean McLeod, the cop she
has fallen in love with. She knows he can do one of two
things: he can turn her in or help her find her mother's
real killer. She feels her future is worth the risk....

JASMINE
CRESSWELL

MIRA

MJC425

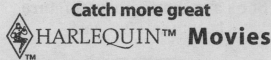
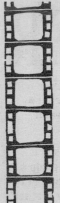

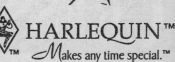